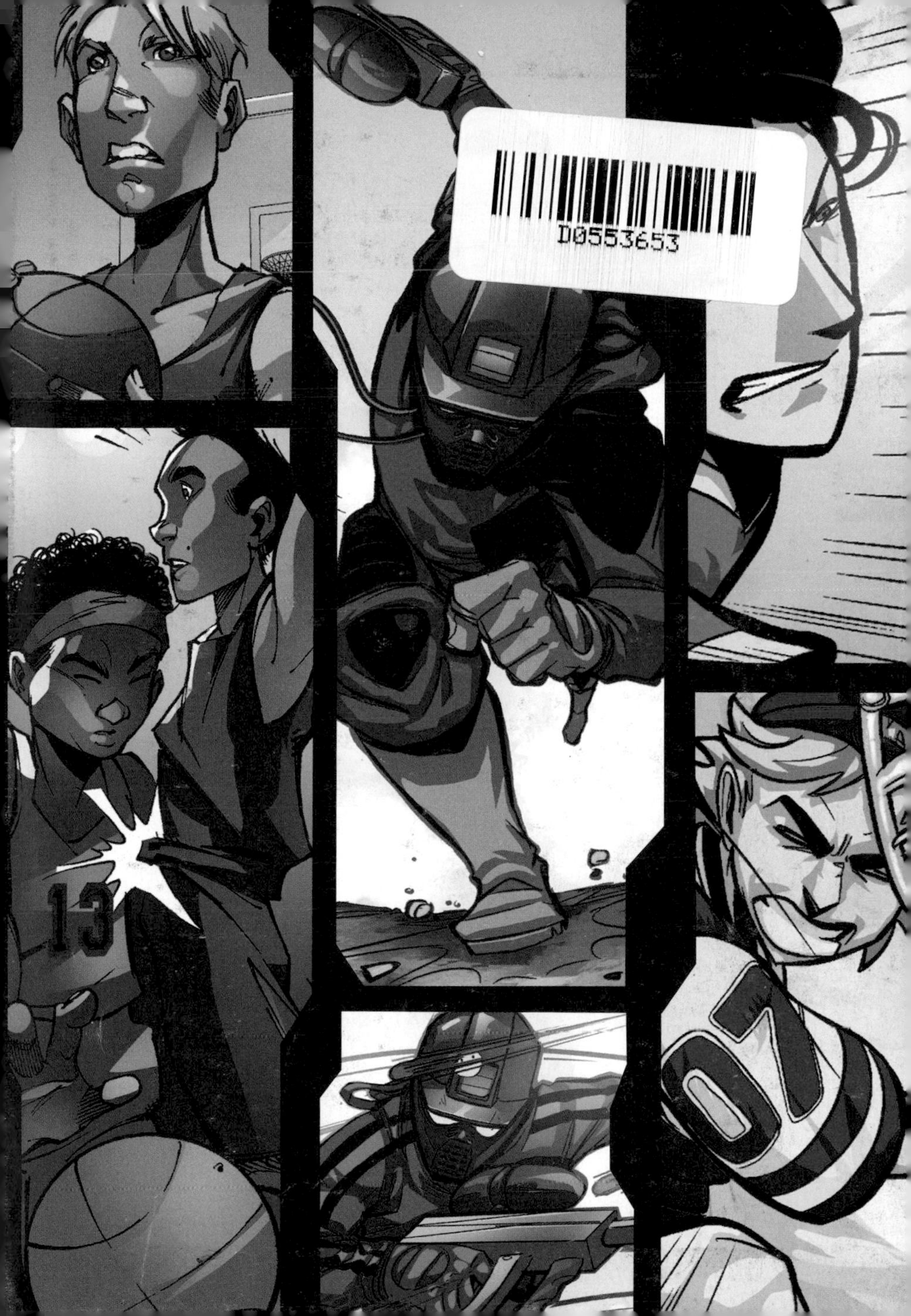
13

UP NEXT ›››

on Sports Illustrated KIDS

:02 SPORTS ZONE SPECIAL REPORT

:04 FEATURE PRESENTATION:

KICKOFF BLITZ

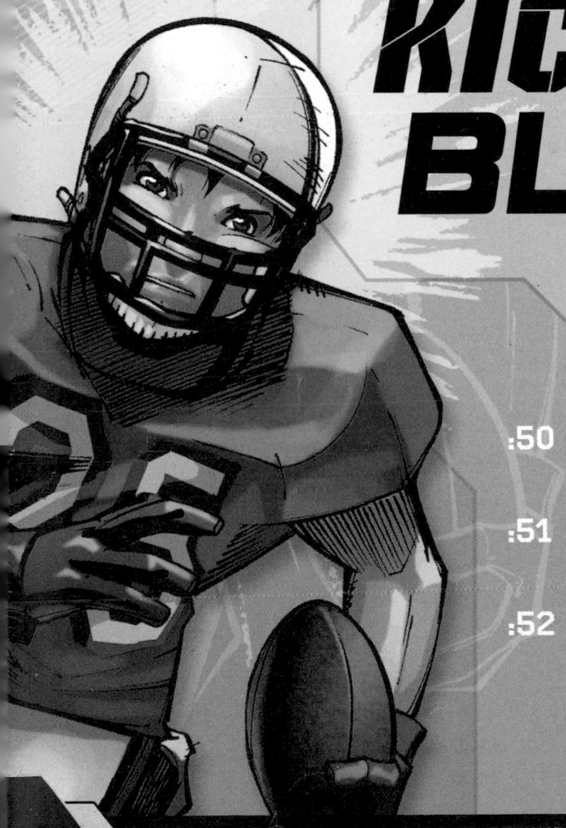

FOLLOWED BY:

:50 SPORTS ZONE POSTGAME RECAP

:51 SPORTS ZONE POSTGAME EXTRA

:52 SI KIDS INFO CENTER

SPECIAL TEAMS PLAY WILL LIKELY DETERMINE THE OUTCOME OF THE WILD SIK TICKER

SPORTS ZONE

SPECIAL REPORT

FBL
FOOTBALL

PNT
PAINTBALL

SKT
SKATEBOARDING

BSL
BASEBALL

BBL
BASKETBALL

HKY

SPECIAL TEAMS ALL-STAR UP AGAINST FORMER TEAM!

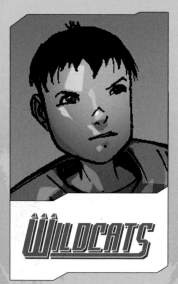

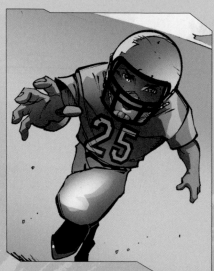

WILDCATS

25

TOU YANG

STATS:
TEAM: WILDCATS
NICKNAME: TINY TOU
AGE: 13
NUMBER: 25
POSITION: SPECIAL TEAMS

BIO: Tou Yang is almost always the smallest player on the field. But, as Coach Michaels says, "It's not the size of the dog in the fight that matters, but rather the size of the fight in the dog that counts." Tou may be tiny, but he leads the league in forced fumbles and total tackles. A former Bandit, Tou will line up against his former bully, Darren, when his Wildcats face off against the Bandits today.

Sports Illustrated KIDS

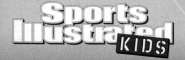

UP NEXT: KICKOFF BLITZ

BLZ vs BKS 3-1
TGR vs RDR 33-32
EAG vs BAN 14-7
SPA vs WLD 4-3
BAN vs RDR 21-15
RZR vs LIG 4-3
BLZ vs BKS 3-1
TGR vs RDR

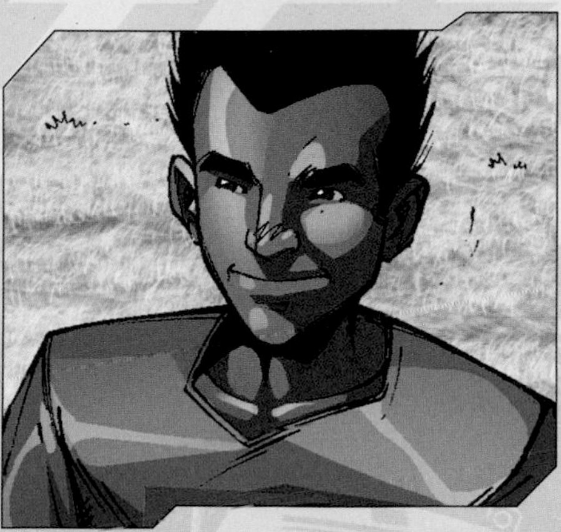

CARLOS RAMIREZ

TEAM: WILDCATS
NUMBER: 7
POSITION: KICKER
BIO: Carlos Ramirez is a soccer standout who was recruited by Coach Michaels to play football. Carlos is the Wildcats' placekicker and punter — and he's also Tou's best friend.

DARREN BROODY

TEAM: BANDITS NUMBER: 46 POSITION: SAFETY
BIO: Darren is quite a bit bigger — and a whole lot meaner — than any other player in the state. He hits like a truck, and never lets up.

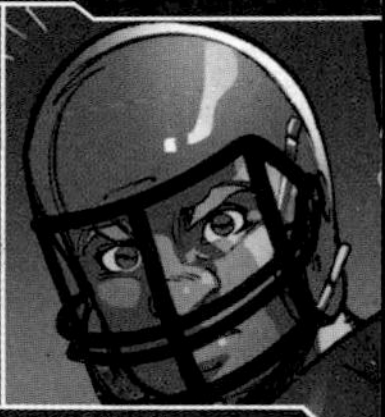

BROODY

TOM MICHAELS

TEAM: WILDCATS POSITION: COACH
BIO: Coach Michaels is calm, cool, and collected. Above all else, he is dedicated to the well-being of his Wildcats on and off the field.

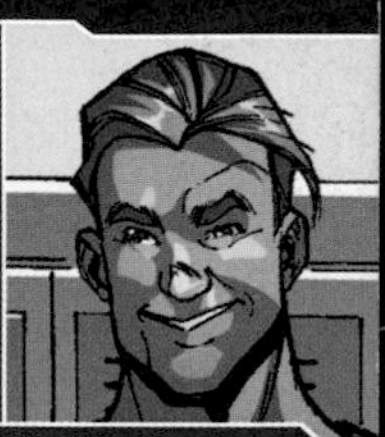

MICHAELS

AARON TURNER

TEAM: BANDITS NUMBER: 12 POSITION: QB
BIO: Aaron is the state's top quarterback. He has an average of 250 yards passing per game, along with 17 touchdowns.

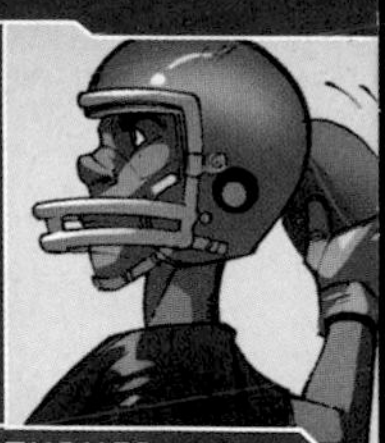

TURNER

'ANG WILL HAVE HIS HANDS FULL AGAINST SUPER-SAFETY DARREN BROODY IN T SIK TICKER

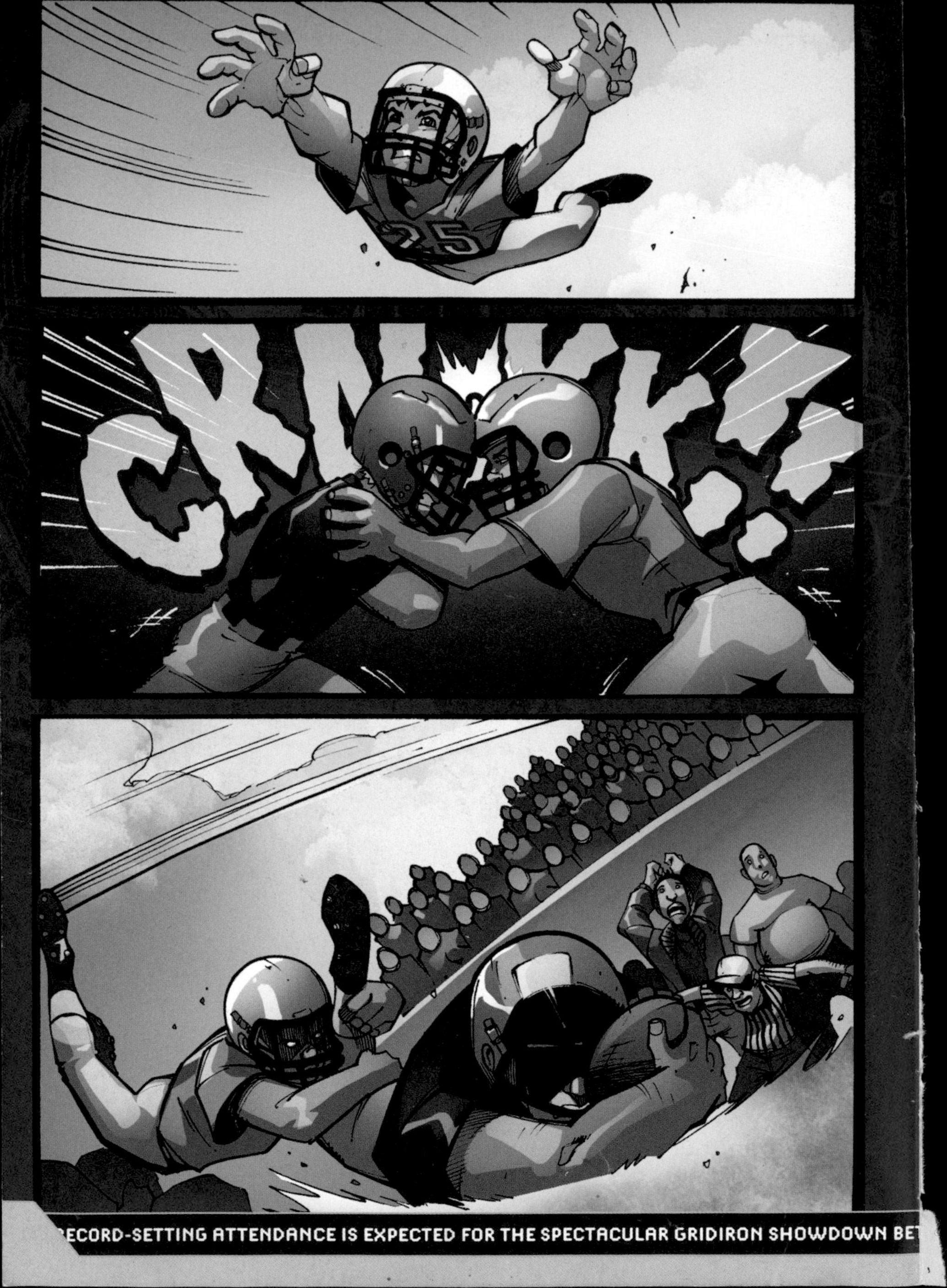

ECORD-SETTING ATTENDANCE IS EXPECTED FOR THE SPECTACULAR GRIDIRON SHOWDOWN BE

Sports Illustrated KIDS

PRESENTS

KICKOFF BLITZ

A PRODUCTION OF

▼▼ STONE ARCH BOOKS
a capstone imprint

written by Blake A. Hoena
illustrated by Alfonso Ruiz
colored by Jorge Gonzalez

designed and directed by Bob Lentz
edited by Sean Tulien
creative direction by Heather Kindseth
editorial direction by Michael Dahl

Sports Illustrated Kids *Kickoff Blitz* is published by Stone Arch Books,
151 Good Counsel Drive, P.O. Box 669,
Mankato, Minnesota 56002.
www.capstonepub.com

Summary: Tou Yang is the smallest kid on his team, but he plays like a
Wildcat. Tou's job is to dash down the field and smash the ballcarrier on
kickoffs and punts, and he does it well. When the Bandits come to town,
an old enemy on the other side of the line goes out of his way to bring Tou
down. Will Tou be able to overcome his gridiron bully, or will Darren send
him to the sidelines?

Cataloging-in-Publication data is available on the Library of Congress
website.
ISBN: 978-1-4342-1909-1 (library binding)
ISBN: 978-1-4342-2292-3 (paperback)

Printed in the United States of America in Stevens Point, Wisconsin.
062011   006248R

'WEEN THE STATE'S TWO HIGHEST-SCORING TEAMS, THE BANDITS AND THE WILDCA   **SIK** *TICKER*

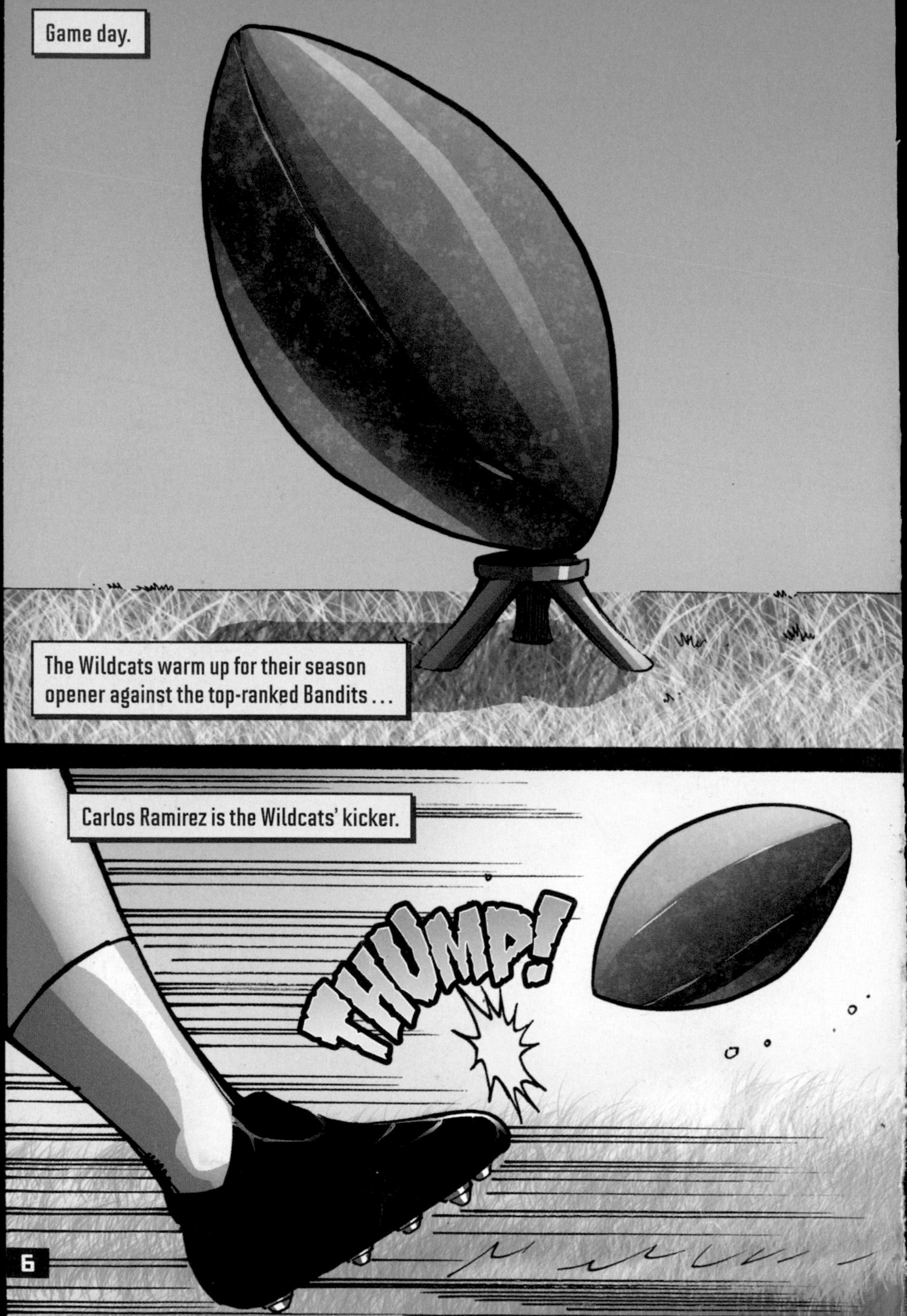
Game day.
The Wildcats warm up for their season opener against the top-ranked Bandits . . .
Carlos Ramirez is the Wildcats' kicker.
THUMP!

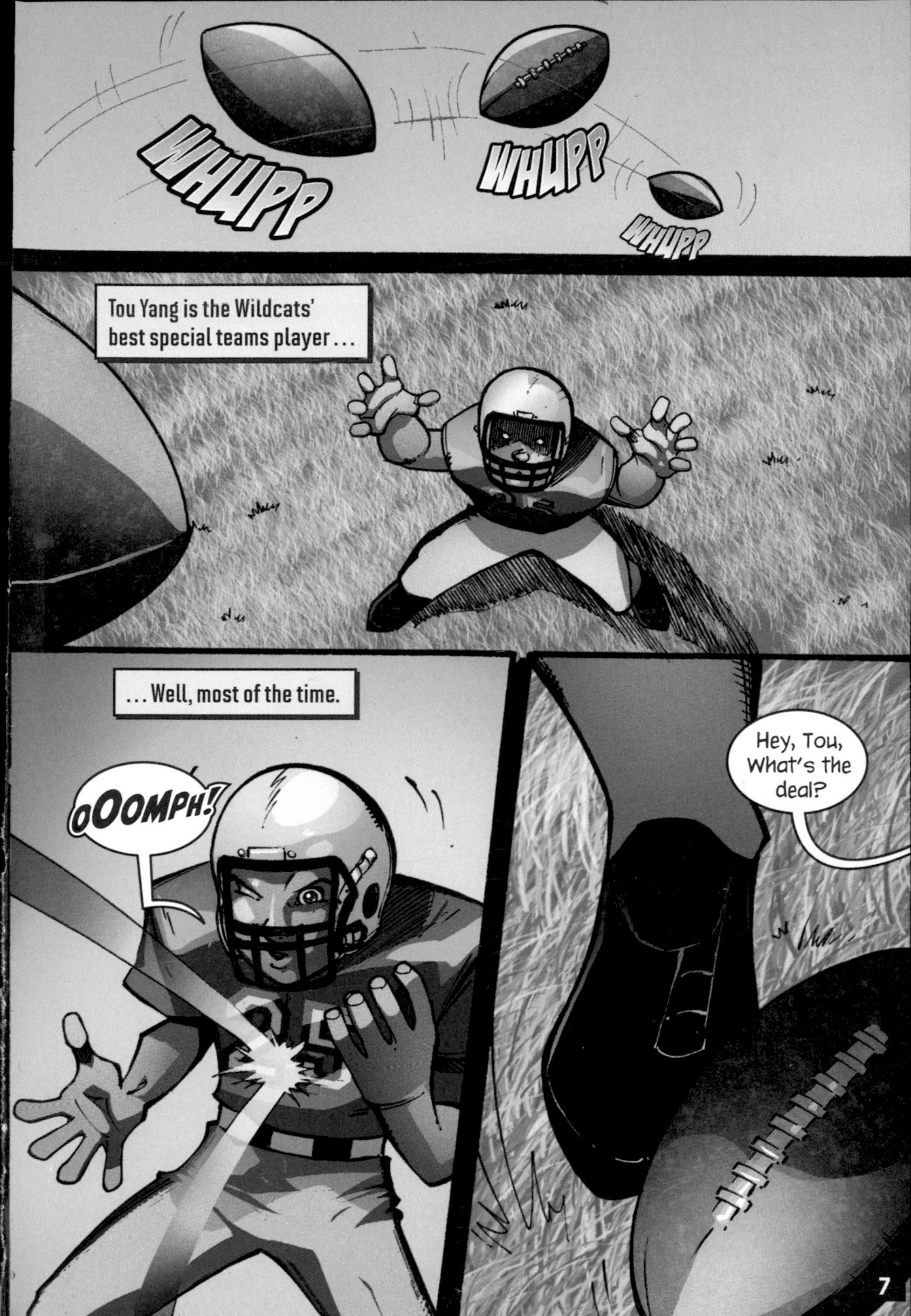
WHUPP
WHUPP
WHUPP
Tou Yang is the Wildcats' best special teams player . . .
. . . Well, most of the time.
OOOMPH!
Hey, Tou, What's the deal?

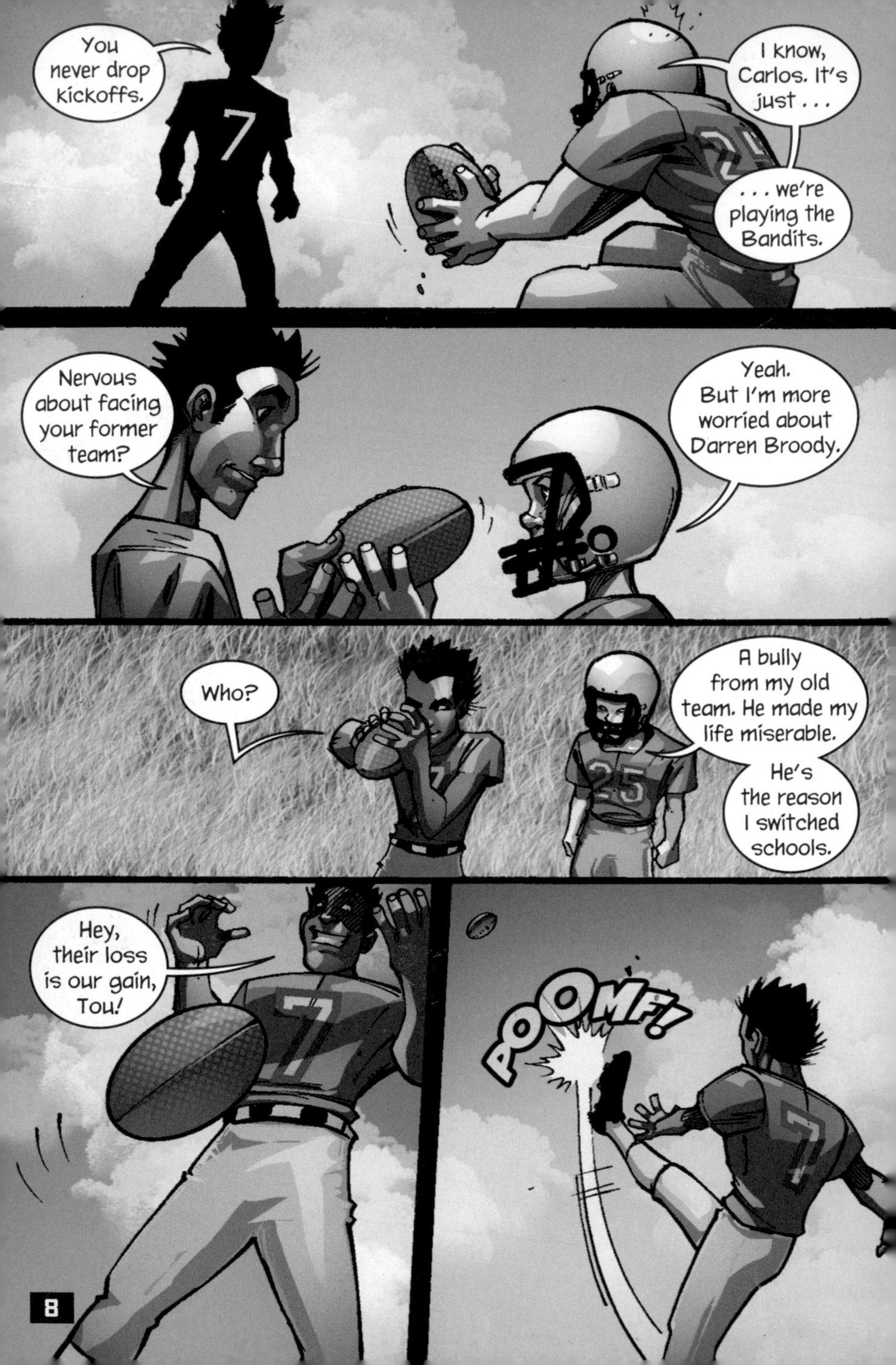
You never drop kickoffs.
I know, Carlos. It's just . . .
. . . we're playing the Bandits.
Nervous about facing your former team?
Yeah. But I'm more worried about Darren Broody.
Who?
A bully from my old team. He made my life miserable.
He's the reason I switched schools.
Hey, their loss is our gain, Tou!
POOMF!

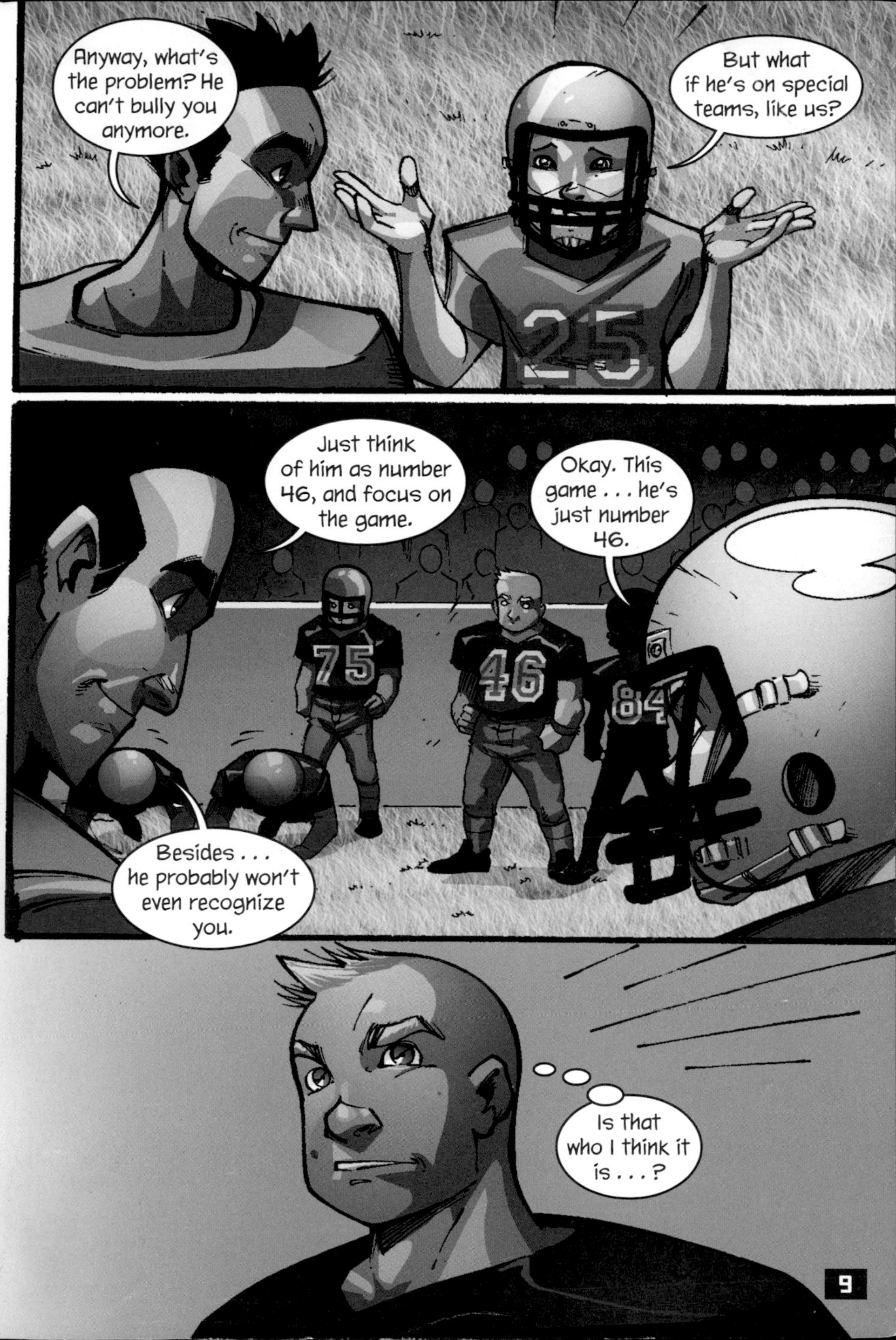
Anyway, what's the problem? He can't bully you anymore.
But what if he's on special teams, like us?
Just think of him as number 46, and focus on the game.
Okay. This game . . . he's just number 46.
Besides . . . he probably won't even recognize you.
Is that who I think it is . . . ?

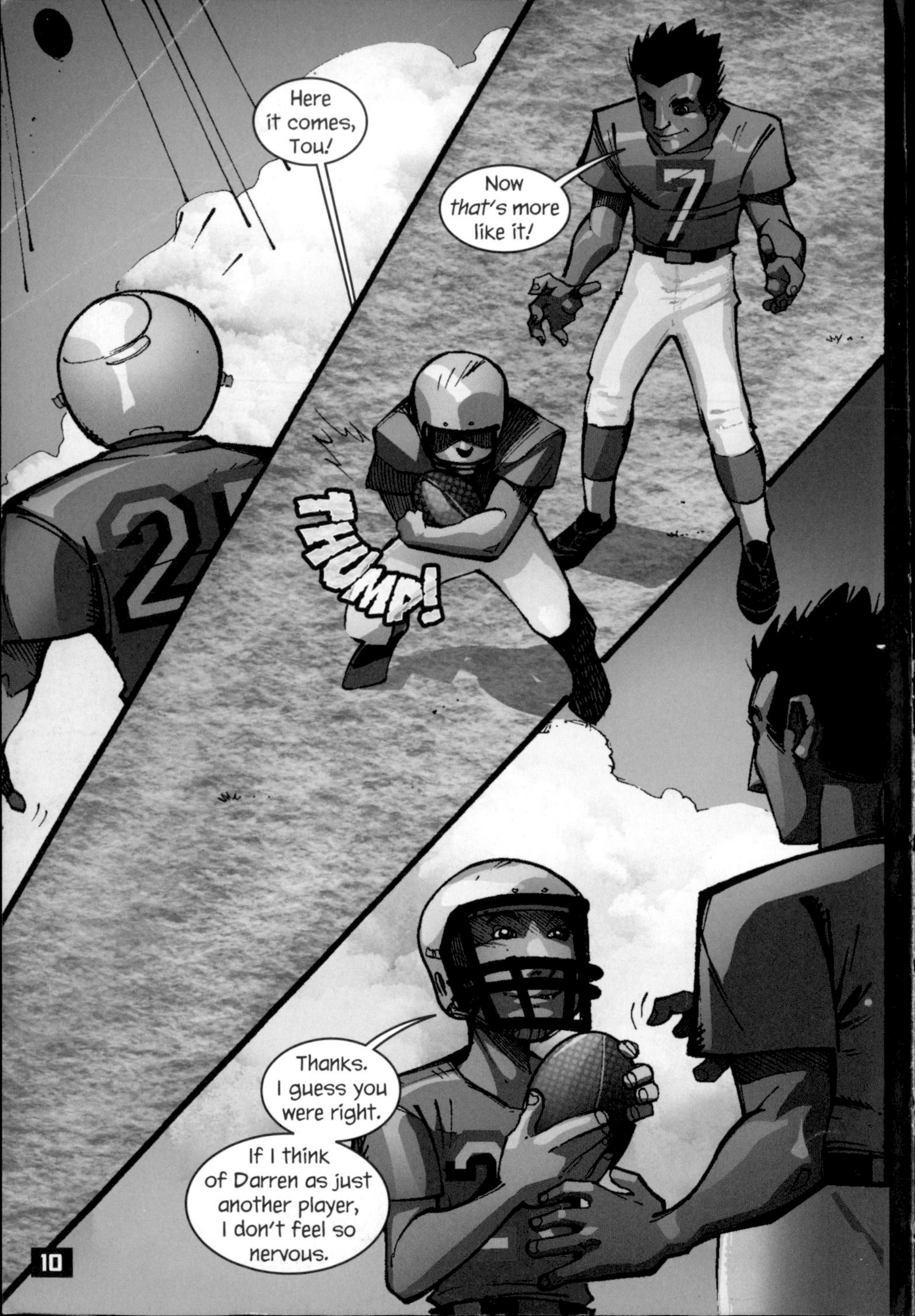
Here it comes, Tou!
Now *that's* more like it!
THUMP!
Thanks. I guess you were right.
If I think of Darren as just another player, I don't feel so nervous.

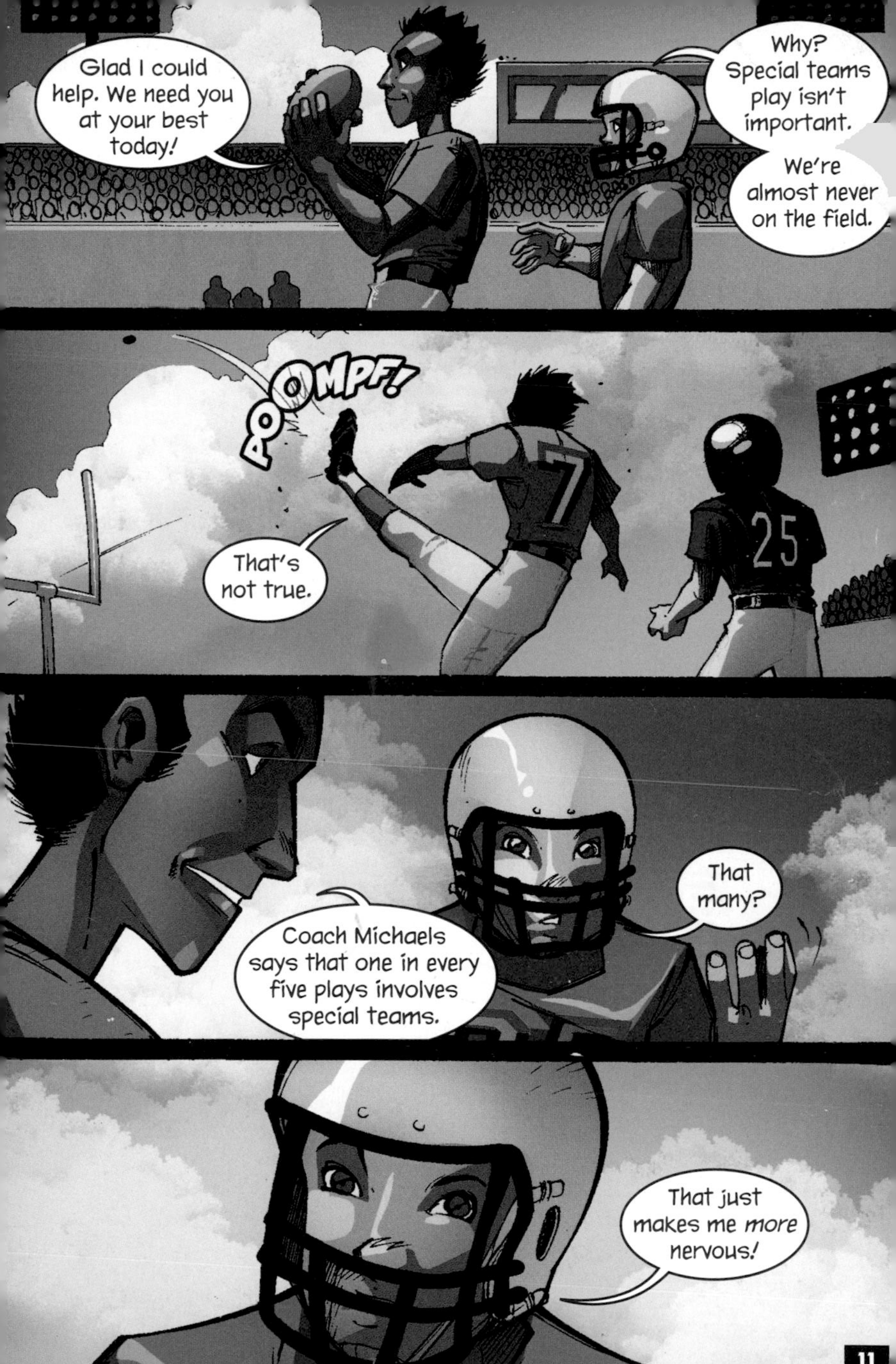
Glad I could help. We need you at your best today!
Why? Special teams play isn't important.
We're almost never on the field.
POOOMPF!
That's not true.
Coach Michaels says that one in every five plays involves special teams.
That many?
That just makes me *more* nervous!

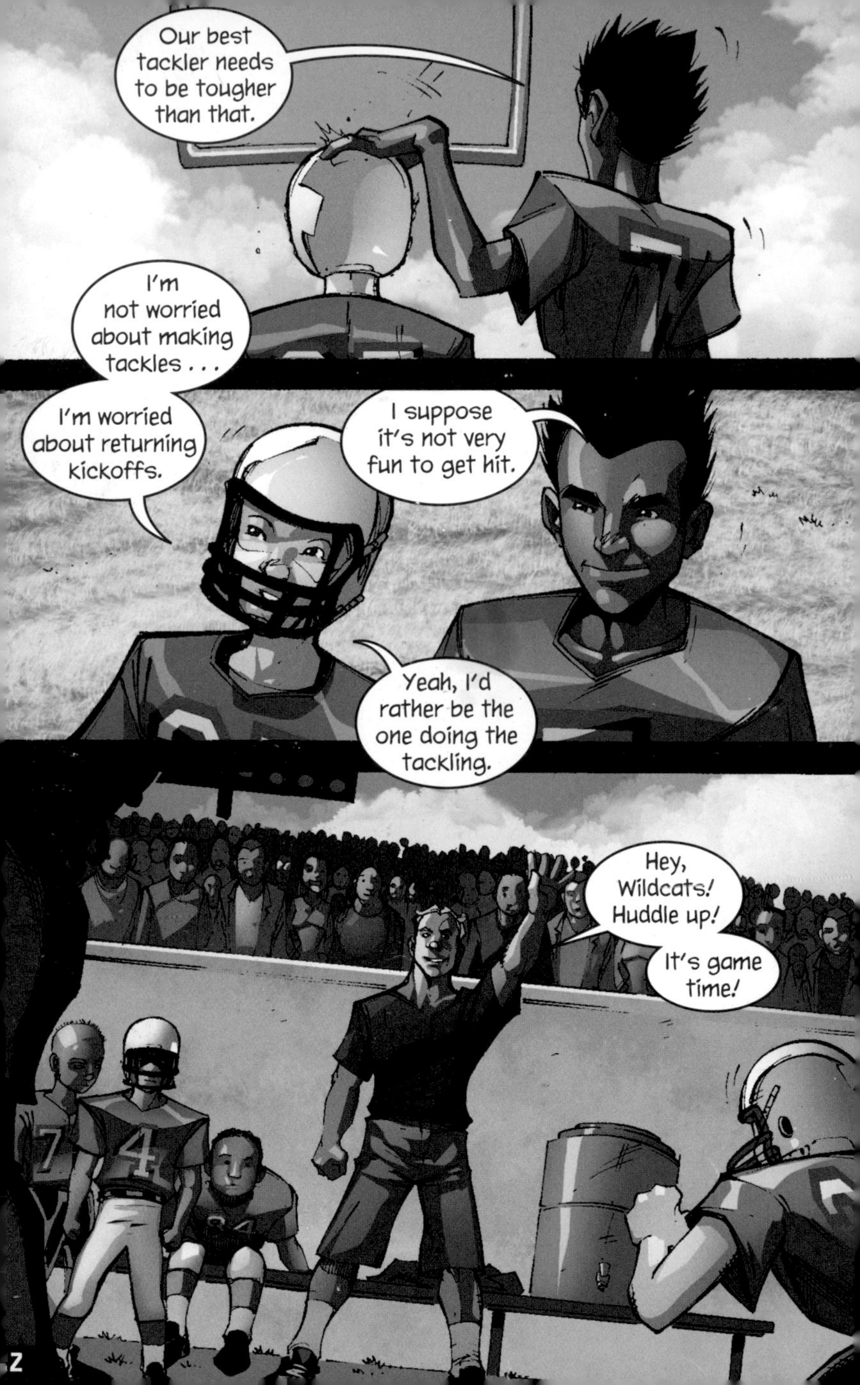
Our best tackler needs to be tougher than that.
I'm not worried about making tackles . . .
I'm worried about returning kickoffs.
I suppose it's not very fun to get hit.
Yeah, I'd rather be the one doing the tackling.
Hey, Wildcats! Huddle up!
It's game time!

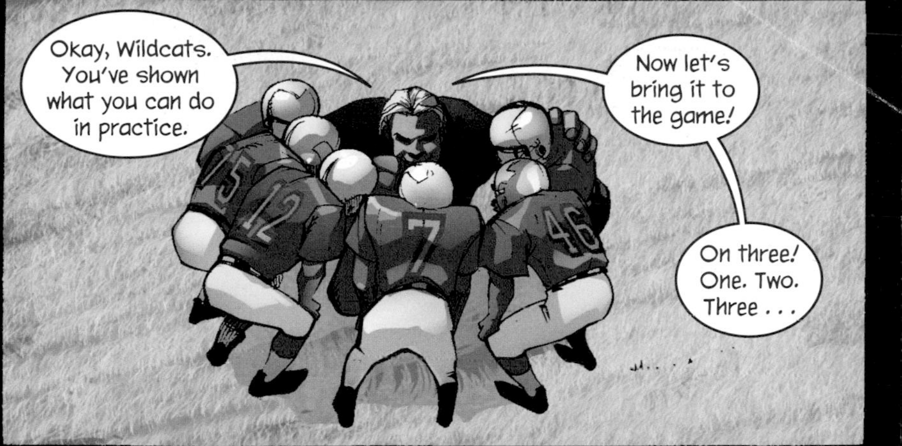
Okay, Wildcats. You've shown what you can do in practice.
Now let's bring it to the game!
On three! One. Two. Three . . .

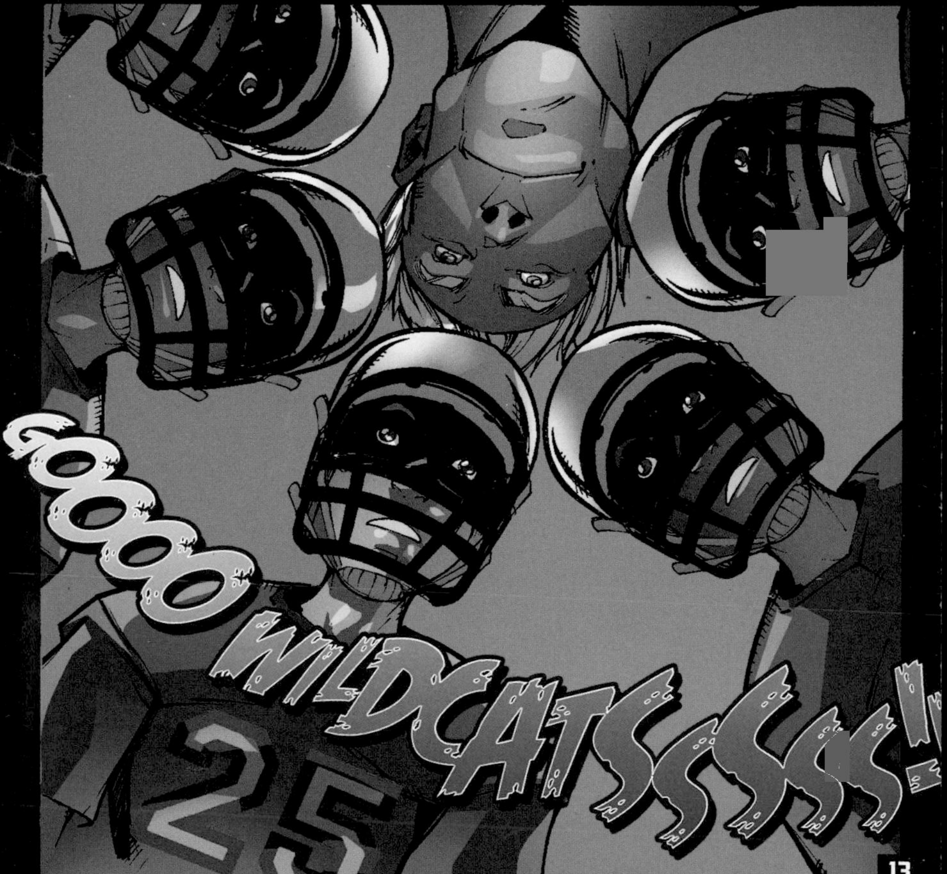
GOOOO WILDCATSSSSS!!

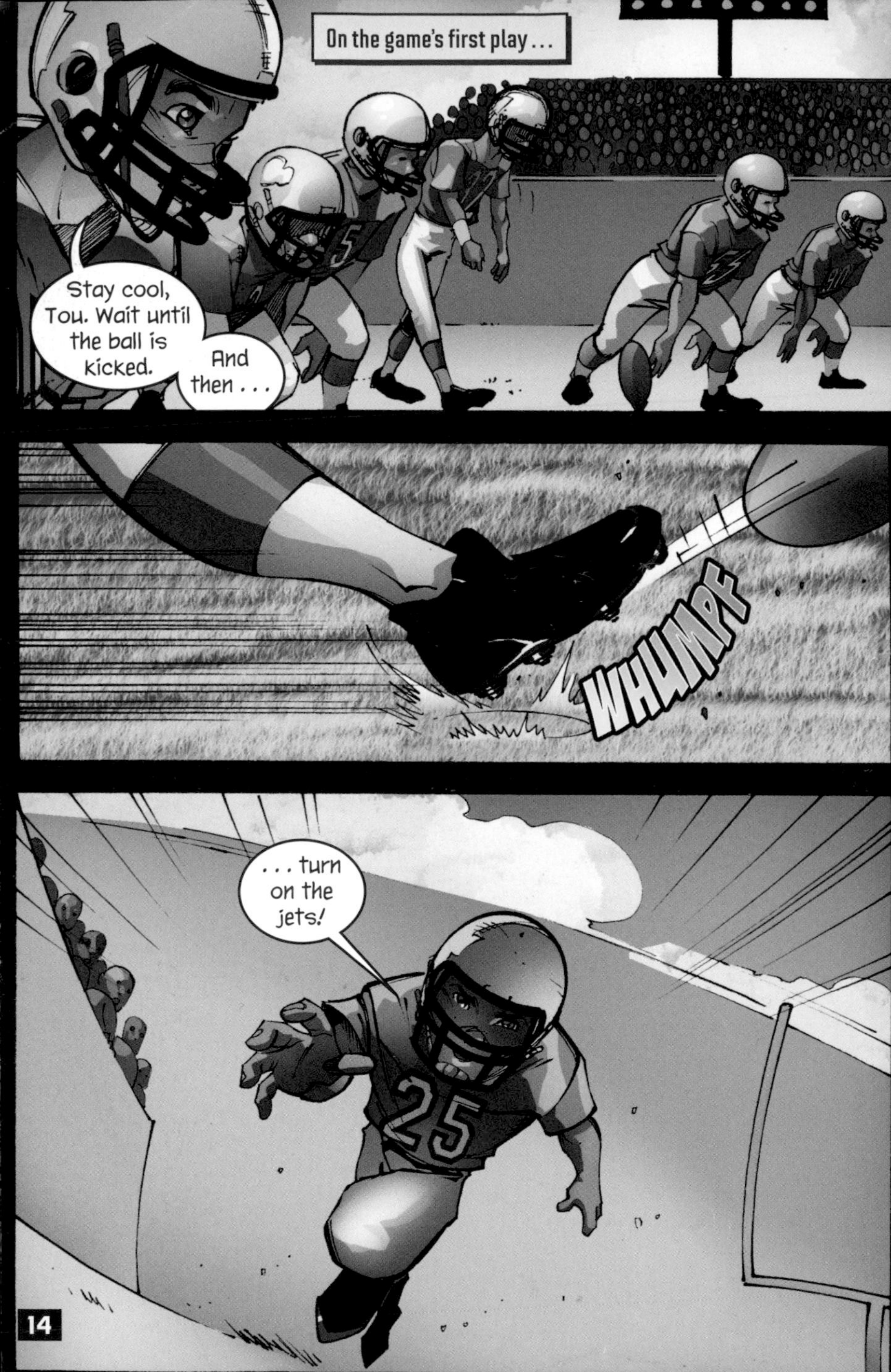
On the game's first play . . .
Stay cool, Tou. Wait until the ball is kicked.
And then . . .
WHUMPF
. . . turn on the jets!

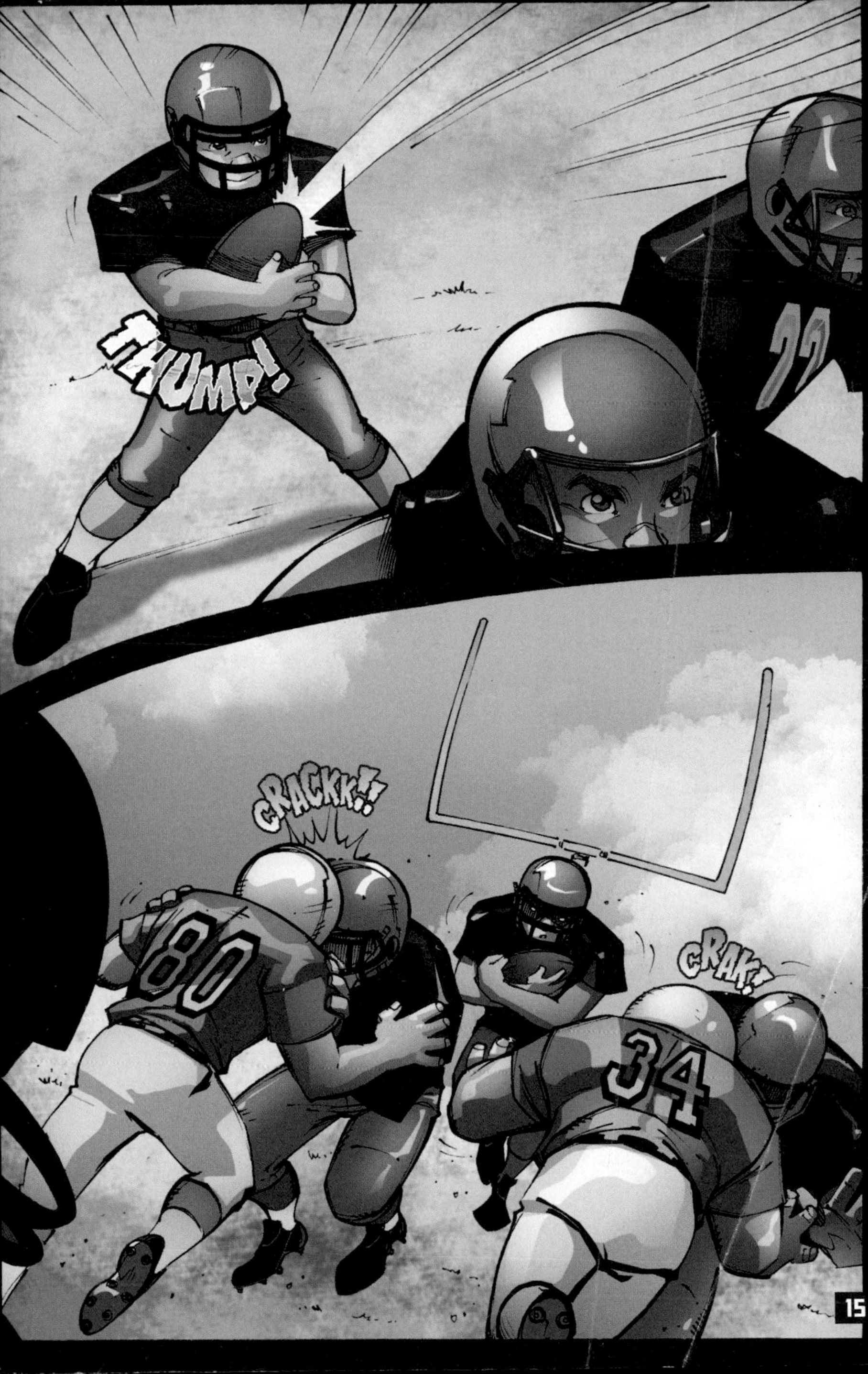
THUMP!
CRACKK!!
CRAK!

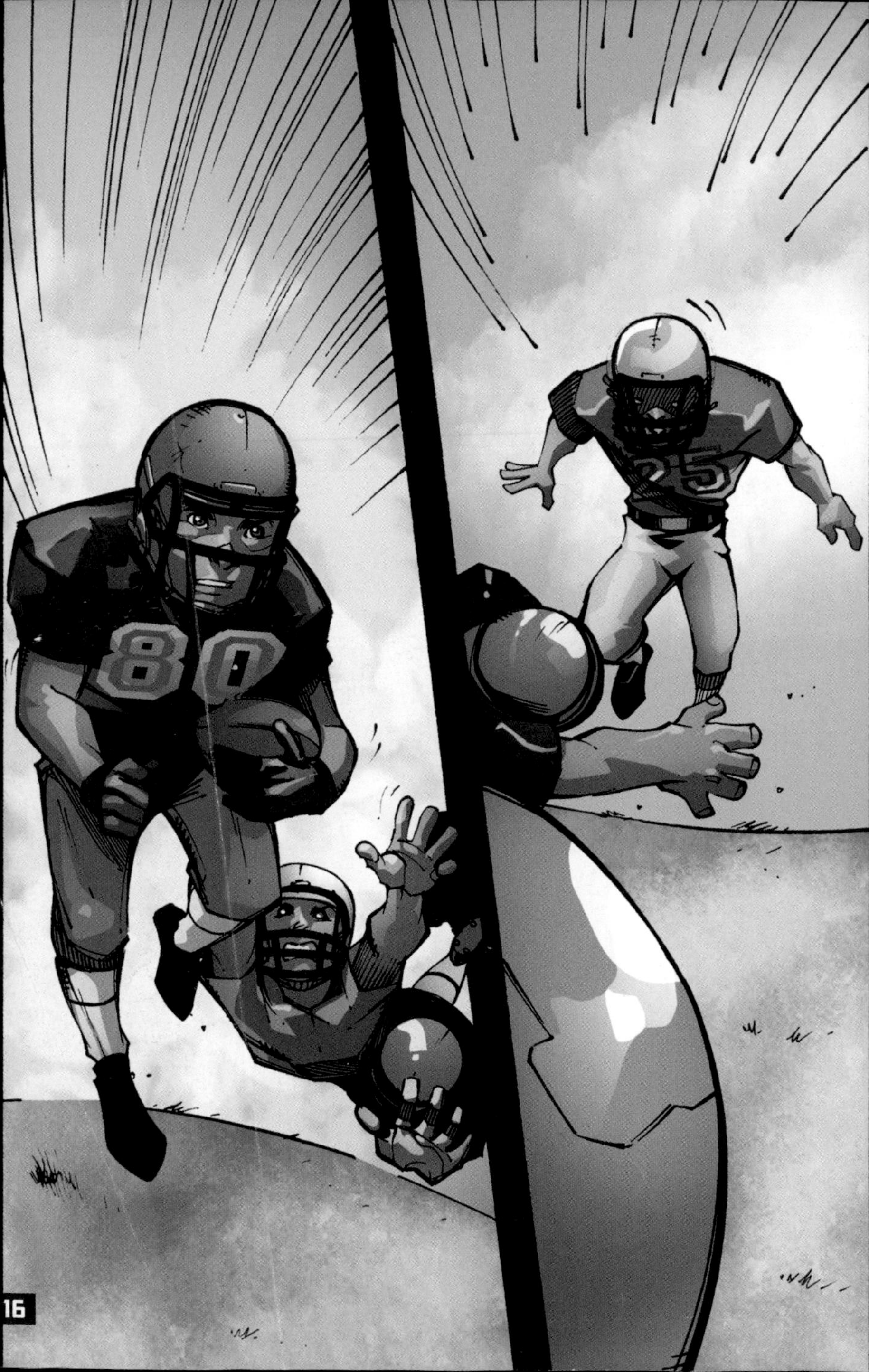
80
25

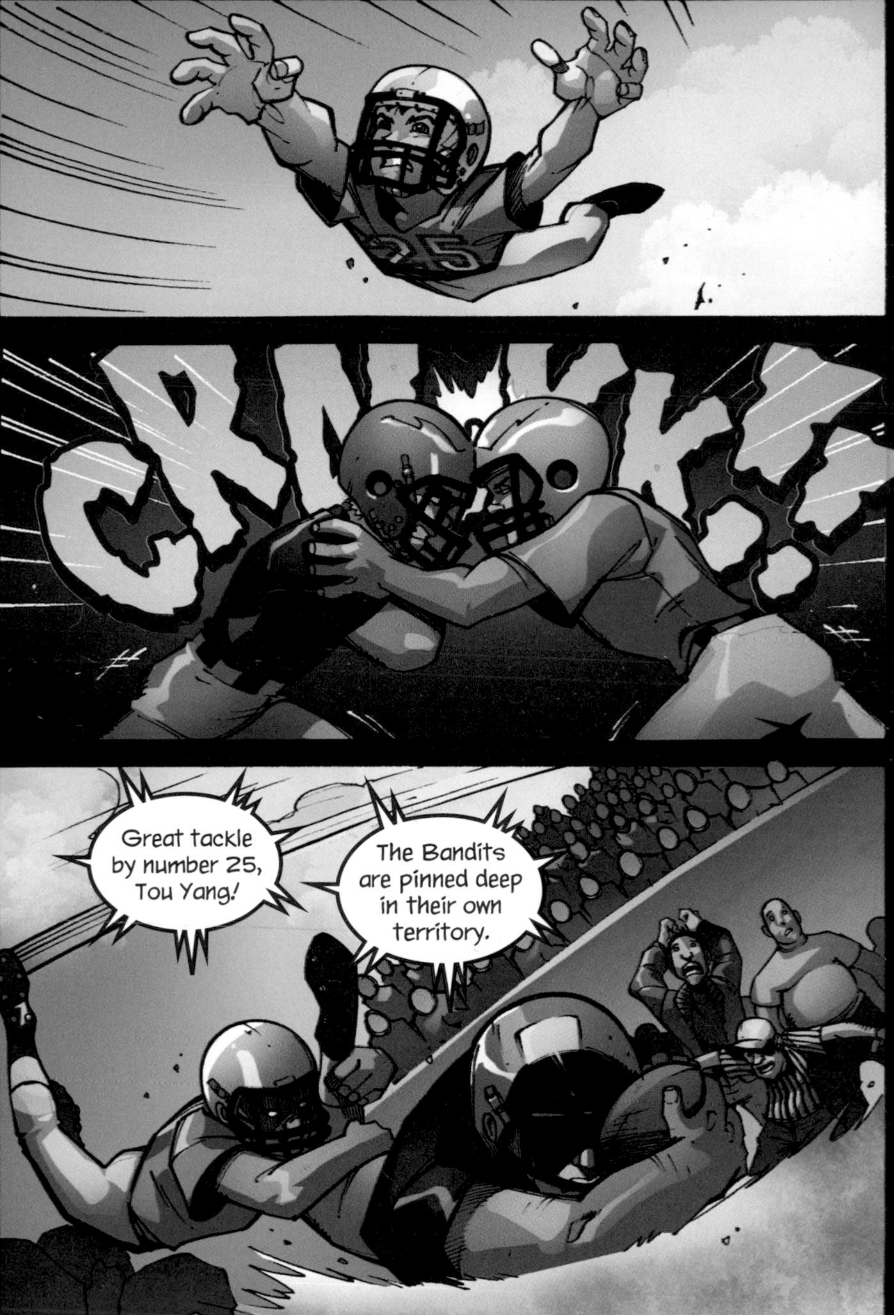
Great tackle by number 25, Tou Yang!
The Bandits are pinned deep in their own territory.

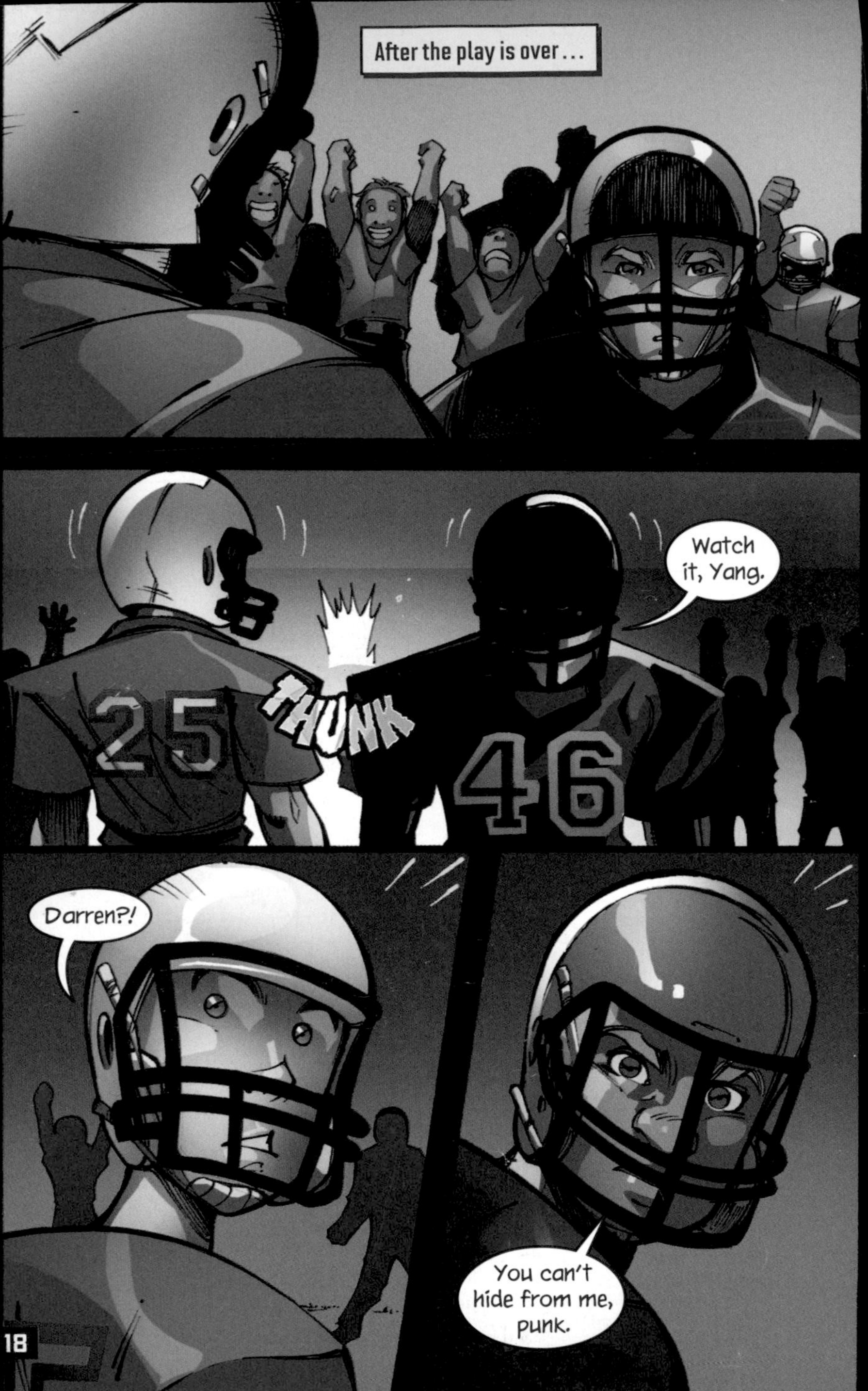
After the play is over...
Watch it, Yang.
THUNK
25
46
Darren?!
You can't hide from me, punk.

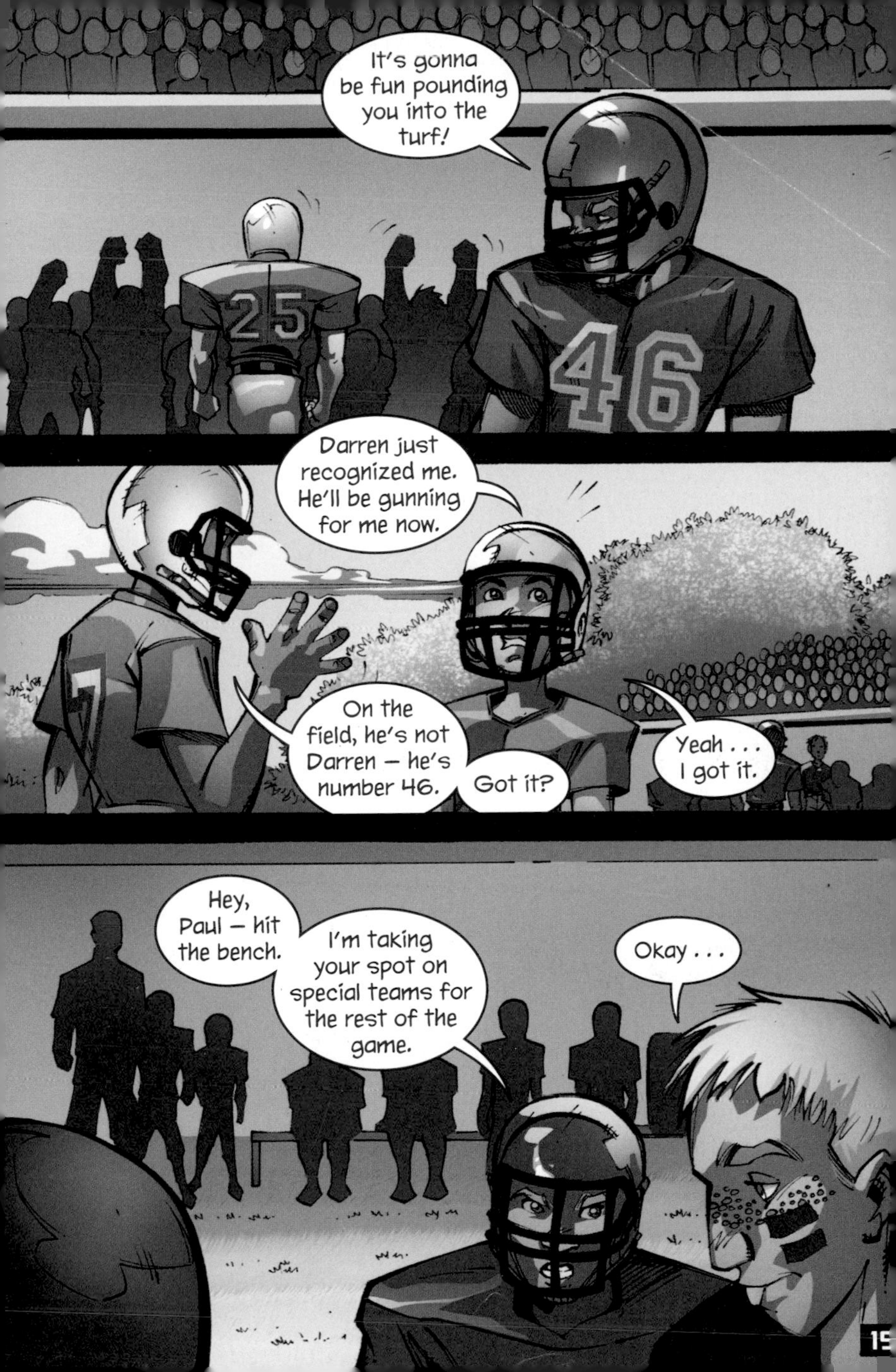
It's gonna be fun pounding you into the turf!
Darren just recognized me. He'll be gunning for me now.
On the field, he's not Darren — he's number 46.
Got it?
Yeah . . . I got it.
Hey, Paul — hit the bench.
I'm taking your spot on special teams for the rest of the game.
Okay . . .

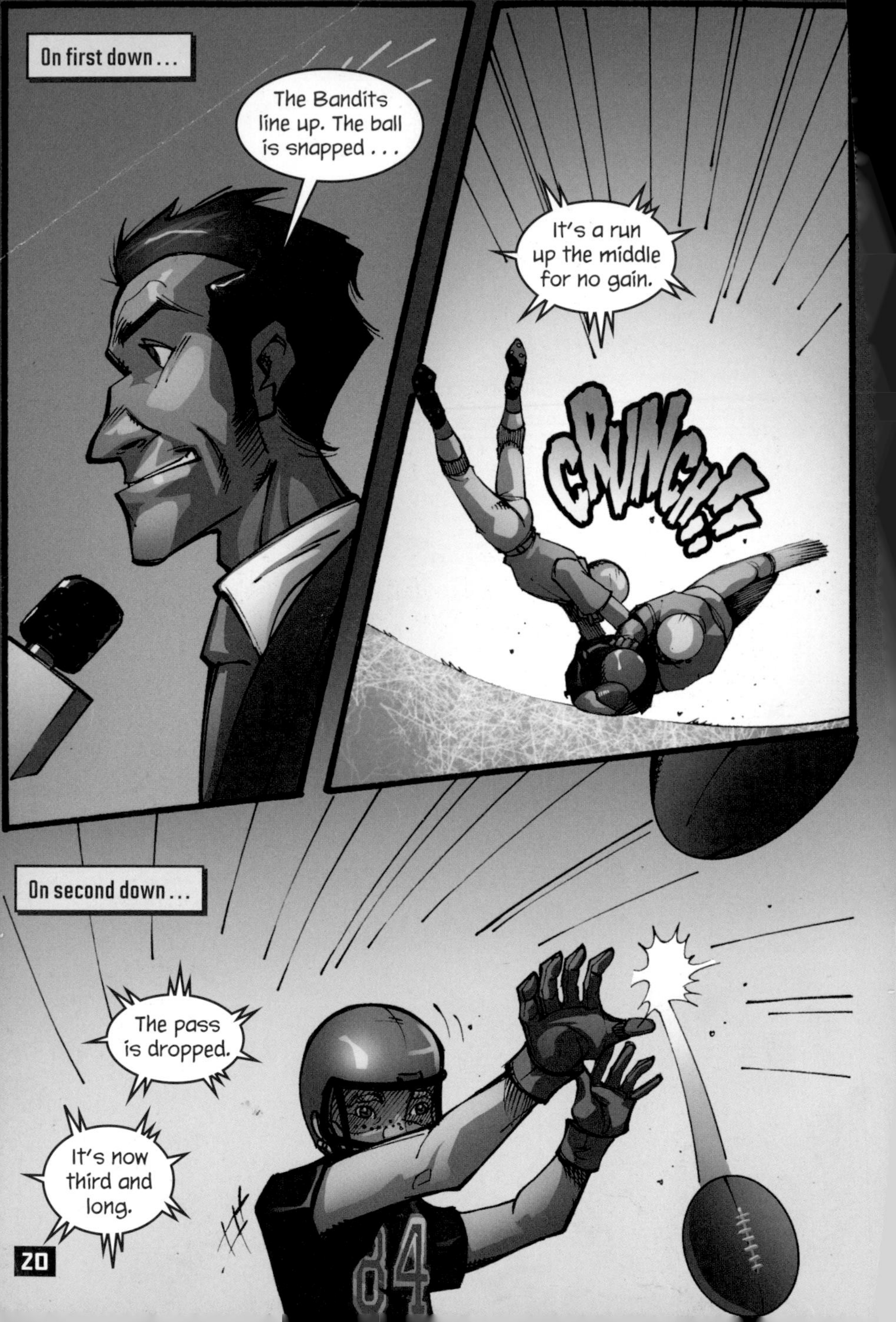
On first down . . .
The Bandits line up. The ball is snapped . . .
It's a run up the middle for no gain.
CRUNCH!!
On second down . . .
The pass is dropped.
It's now third and long.
84

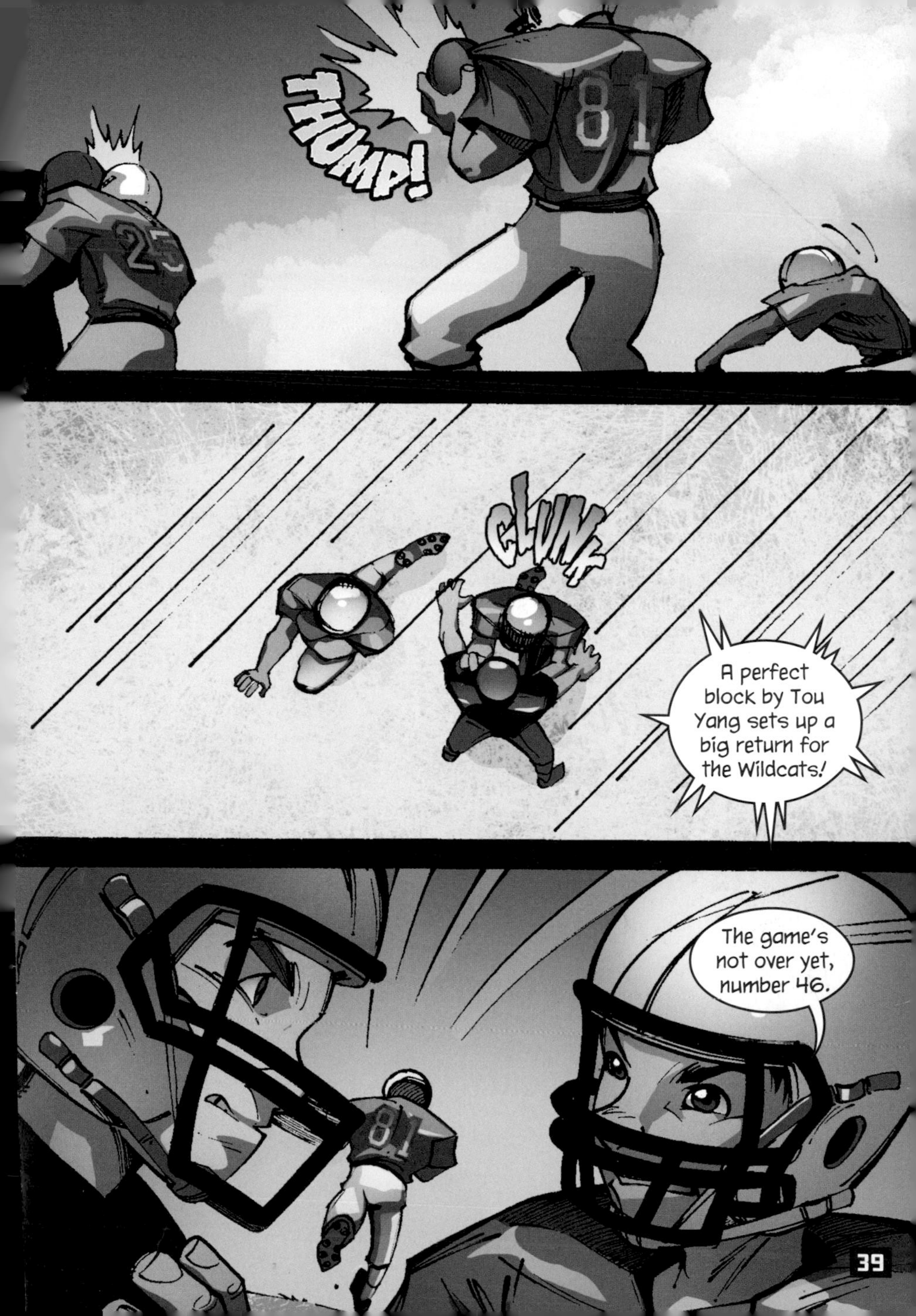
THUMP!
CLUNK
A perfect block by Tou Yang sets up a big return for the Wildcats!
The game's not over yet, number 46.

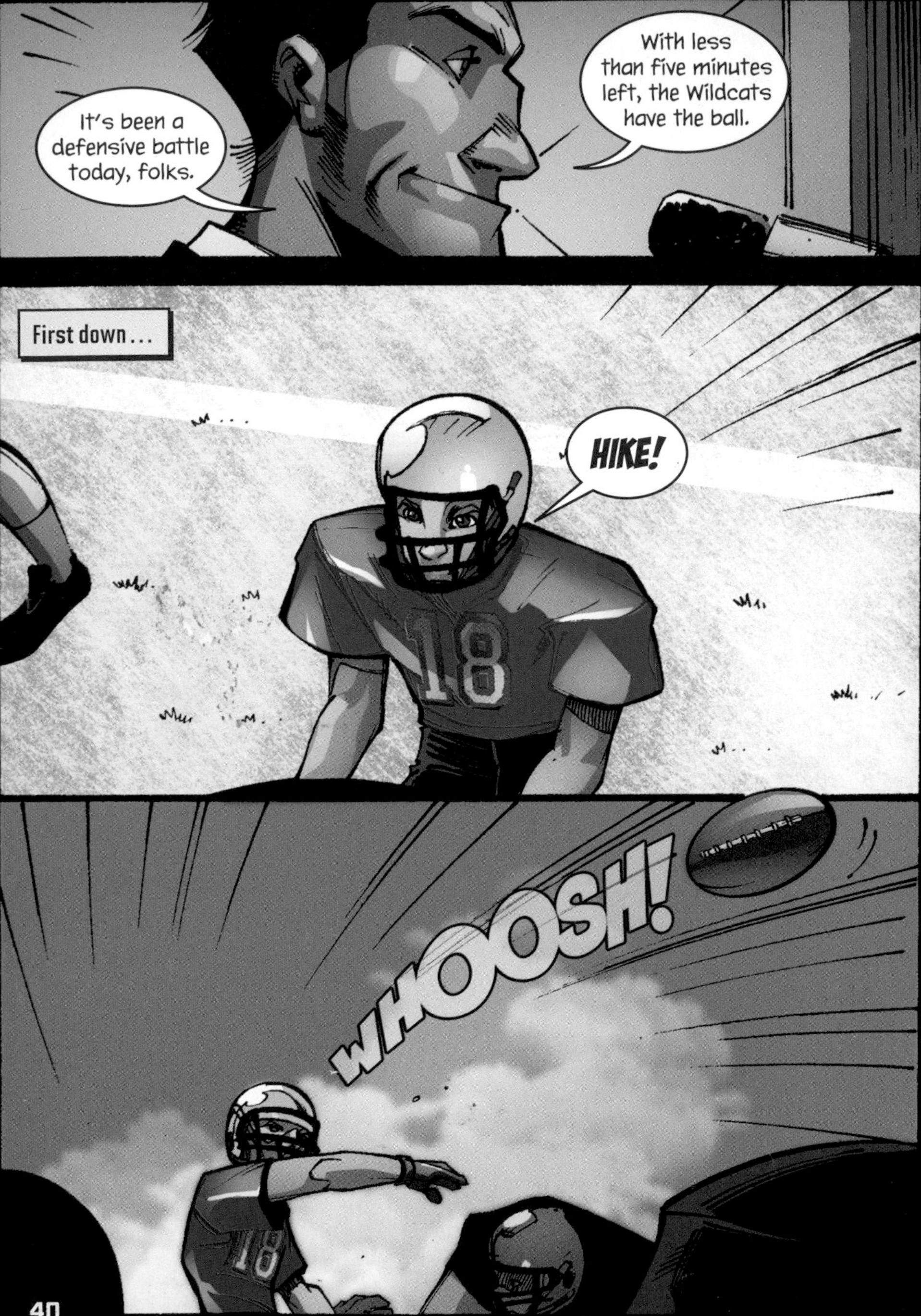
It's been a defensive battle today, folks.
With less than five minutes left, the Wildcats have the ball.
First down . . .
HIKE!
WHOOSH!

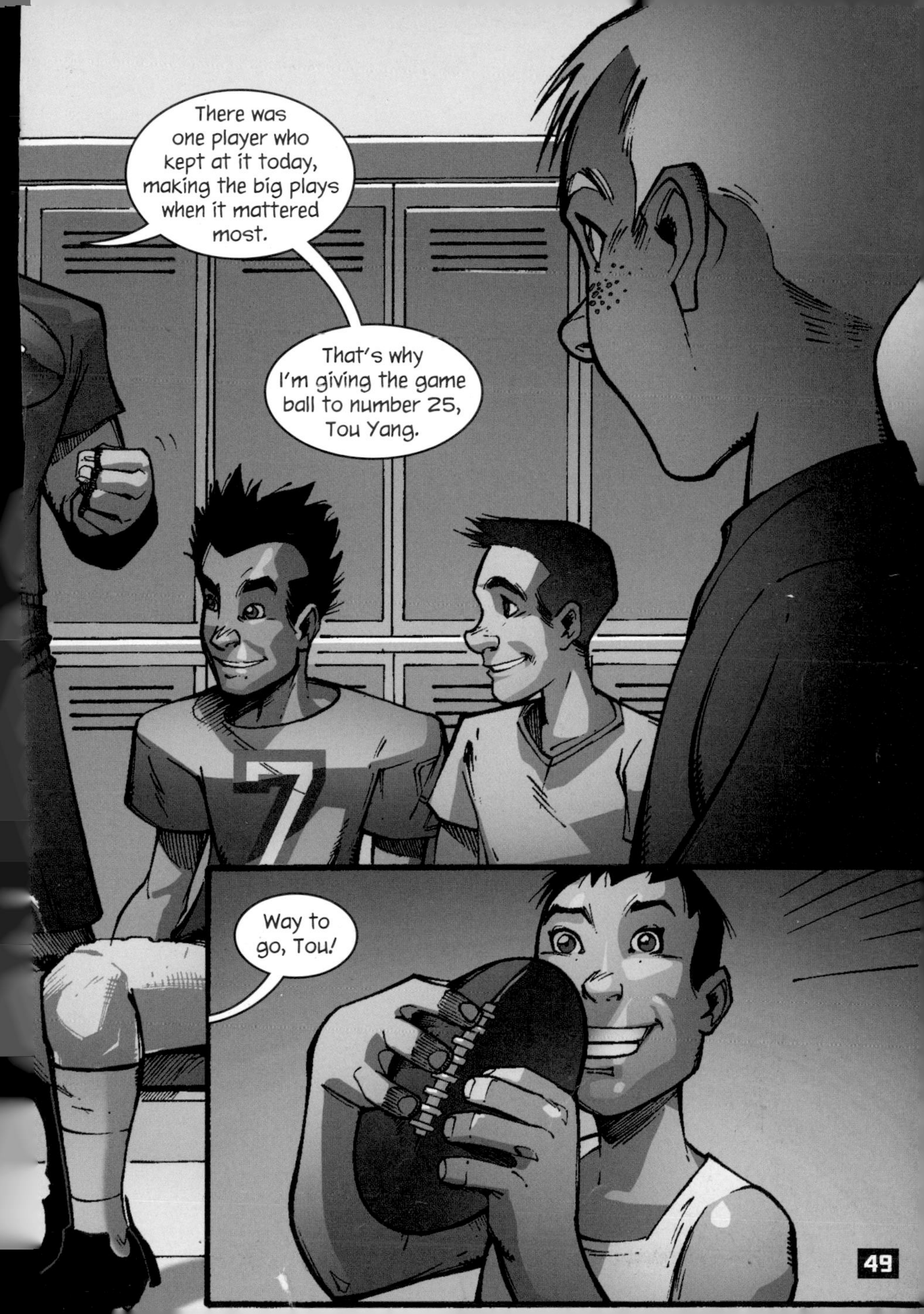
There was one player who kept at it today, making the big plays when it mattered most.
That's why I'm giving the game ball to number 25, Tou Yang.
Way to go, Tou!

SPORTS ZONE

POSTGAME RECAP

FBL FOOTBALL
PNT PAINTBALL
SKT SKATEBOARDING
BSL BASEBALL
BBL BASKETBALL
HKY HOCKEY

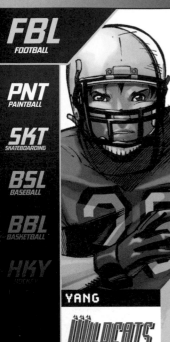

YANG

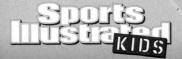

WILDCATS

WILDCATS BEAT THE BANDITS WITH A LAST-SECOND TRICK PLAY!

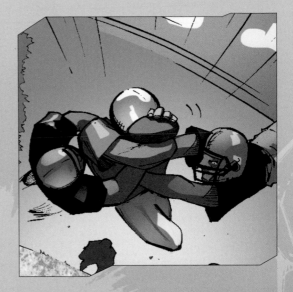

BY THE NUMBERS

FINAL SCORE:
WILDCATS: 10
BANDITS: 7

GAME HIGHS:
TACKLES: YANG, 9
FIELD GOALS: RAMIREZ, 1
PENALTIES: BROODY, 4

STORY: Special-teams standout Tou Yang shocked every single fan when he scored the game-winning touchdown against the Bandits today. The risky play was a stroke of brilliance by Coach Michaels, since no one expected "Tiny" Tou to catch a pass thrown by the punter, Carlos Ramirez. The Bandits' safety, Darren Broody, was quoted as saying "Tou may be a little runt, but boy, does that kid hit hard."

Sports Illustrated KIDS

UP NEXT: SI KIDS INFO CENTER

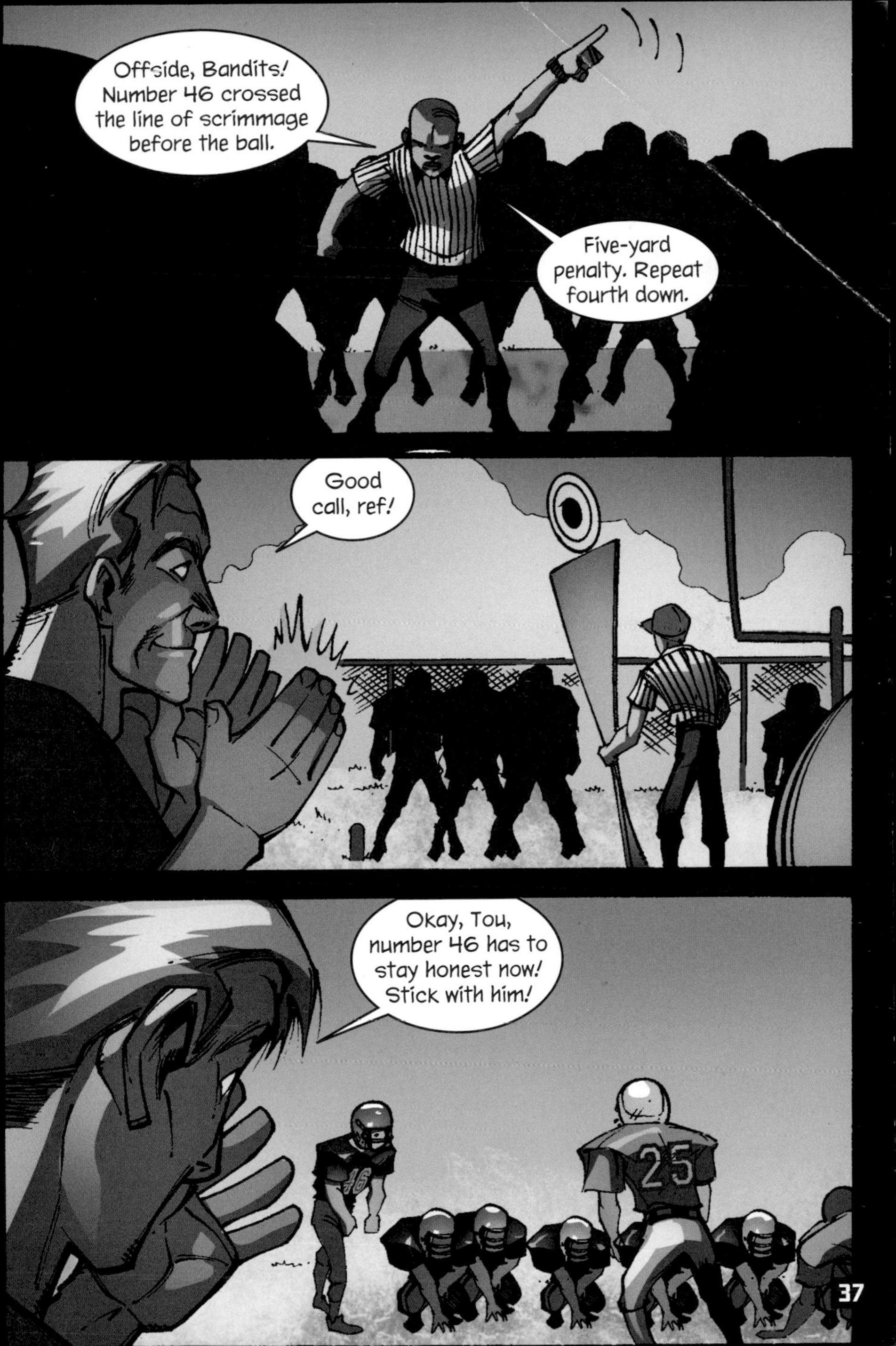
Offside, Bandits! Number 46 crossed the line of scrimmage before the ball.
Five-yard penalty. Repeat fourth down.
Good call, ref!
Okay, Tou, number 46 has to stay honest now! Stick with him!
25
46

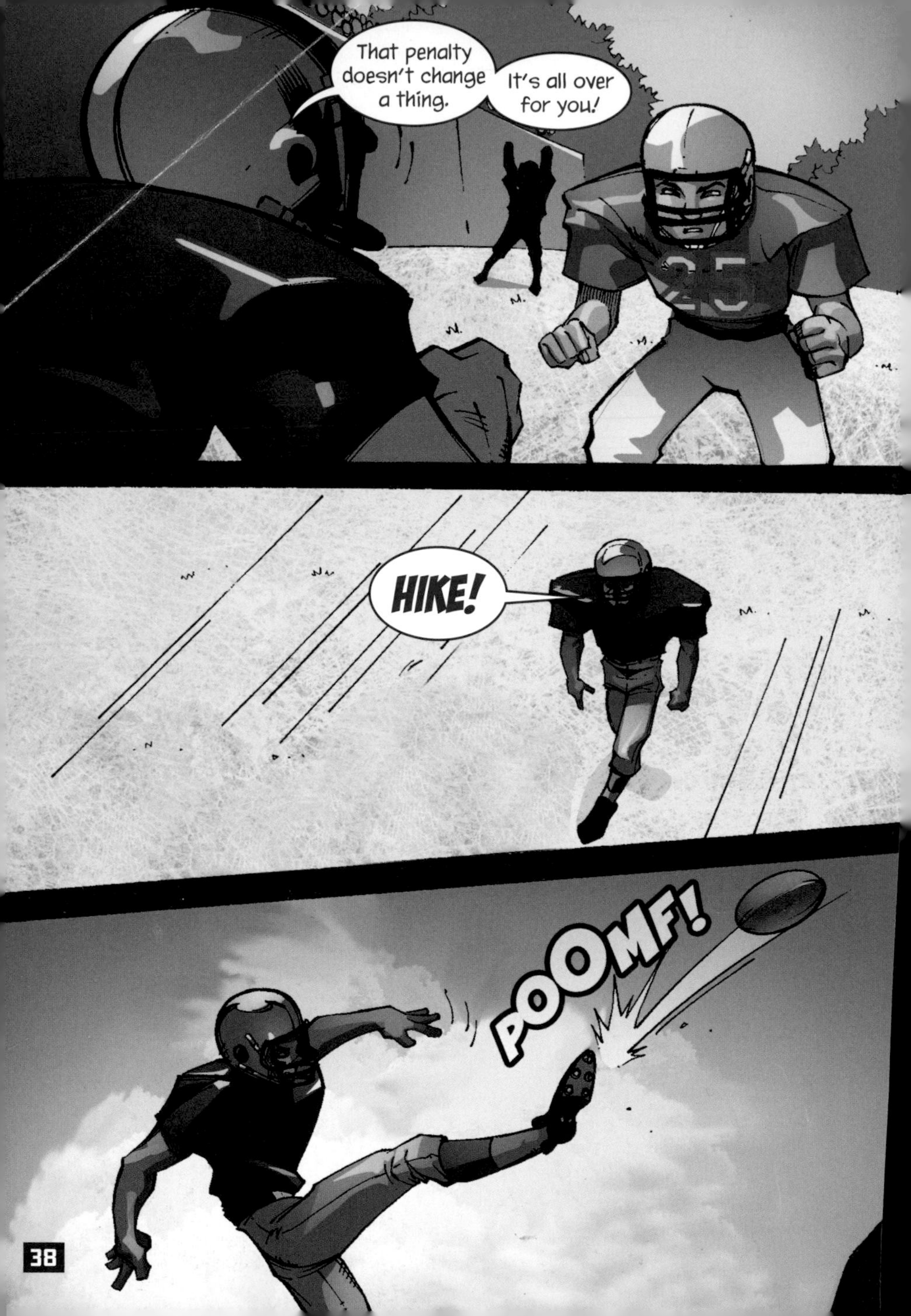
That penalty doesn't change a thing.
It's all over for you!
HIKE!
POOMF!

SZ POSTGAME EXTRA

WHERE *YOU* ANALYZE THE GAME!

BLZ vs BNS
3-1
TGR vs RDR
33-32
FAG vs BAN
14-7
SPA vs WLD
4-3
BAN vs WLD
21-15
RDR vs LIG
4-3
BLZ vs BNS
3-1

Football fans went wild today when Tou Yang and the Wildcats outgunned the Bandits. Let's go into the stands and ask some fans for their perspectives on today's exciting game...

DISCUSSION QUESTION 1

Tou is the smallest player on the Wildcats, but that doesn't stop him from making big plays. How much does size matter in sports?

DISCUSSION QUESTION 2

Carlos Ramirez hopes to one day play professional soccer. If you could play any sport professionally, which sport would you choose? Why?

WRITING PROMPT 1

Tou has to handle the pressures of a bully *and* a big football game. When was the last time you felt pressure? How did you handle it? Write about it.

WRITING PROMPT 2

Carlos throws the winning touchdown in a big game. When was the last time you did something you were proud of? What happened? Write about it.

GLOSSARY

COVERAGE (KUHV-rij)—a defensive scheme designed to stop the pass, or a special-teams scheme designed to limit a kick return

LINE OF SCRIMMAGE (LINE UHV SKRIM-ij)—an invisible line that stretches across the field, separating both teams prior to the snap of the ball

MISERABLE (MIZ-ur-uh-buhl)—very sad, unhappy, uncomfortable, or dejected

OFFSIDE (awf-SIDE)—a penalty called when a player is on the wrong side of the line of scrimmage when the ball is snapped

RECOGNIZE (REK-uhg-nize)—to see someone and to know who the person is

RUNT (RUHNT)—the smallest or weakest member of a group. It is sometimes used as an insult directed at small people.

SPECIAL TEAMS (SPESH-uhl TEEMZ)—groups of players who are on the field during kicks and punts

VICIOUS (VISH-uhss)—cruel and mean, or fierce and dangerous

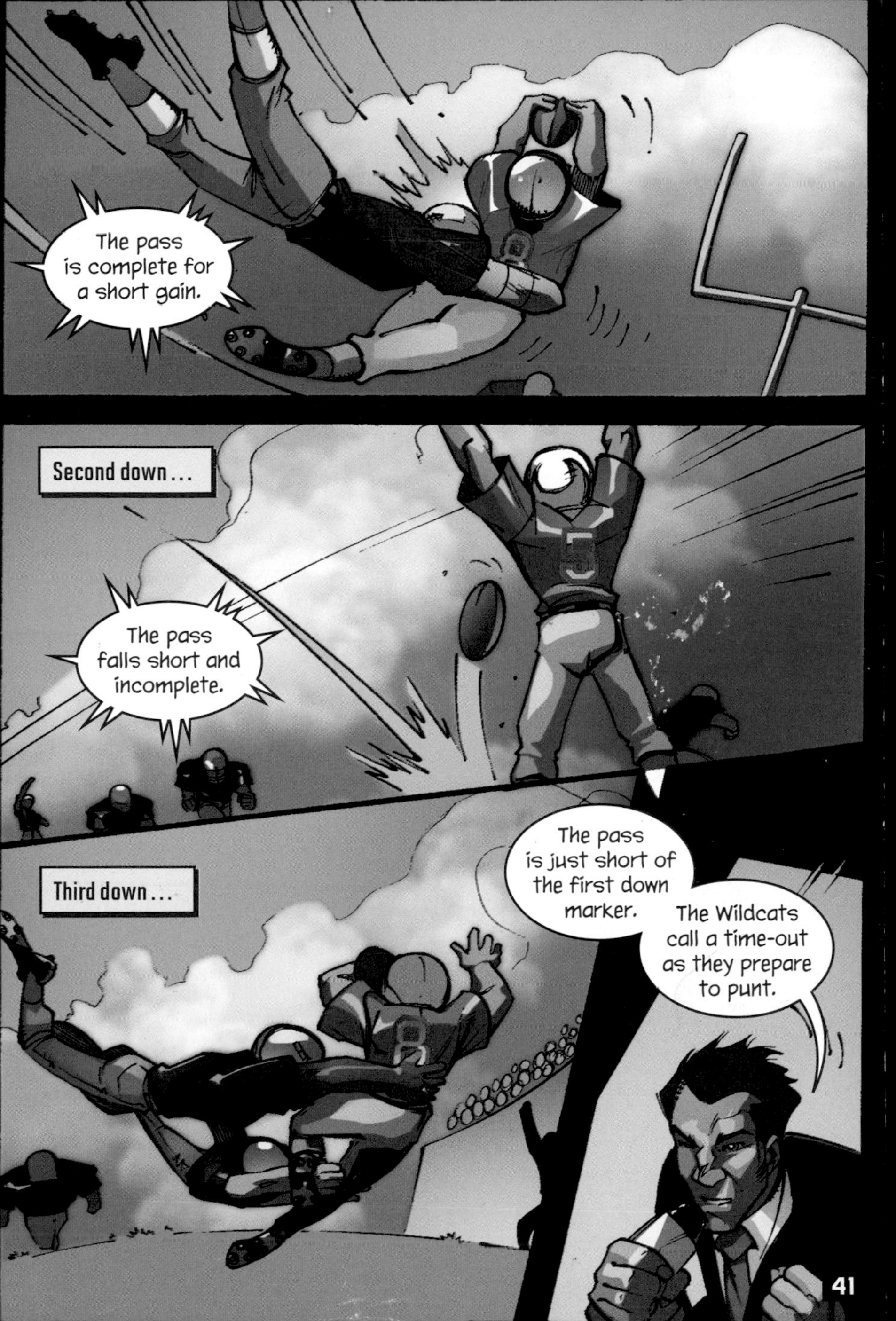

The pass is complete for a short gain.
Second down...
The pass falls short and incomplete.
Third down...
The pass is just short of the first down marker.
The Wildcats call a time-out as they prepare to punt.

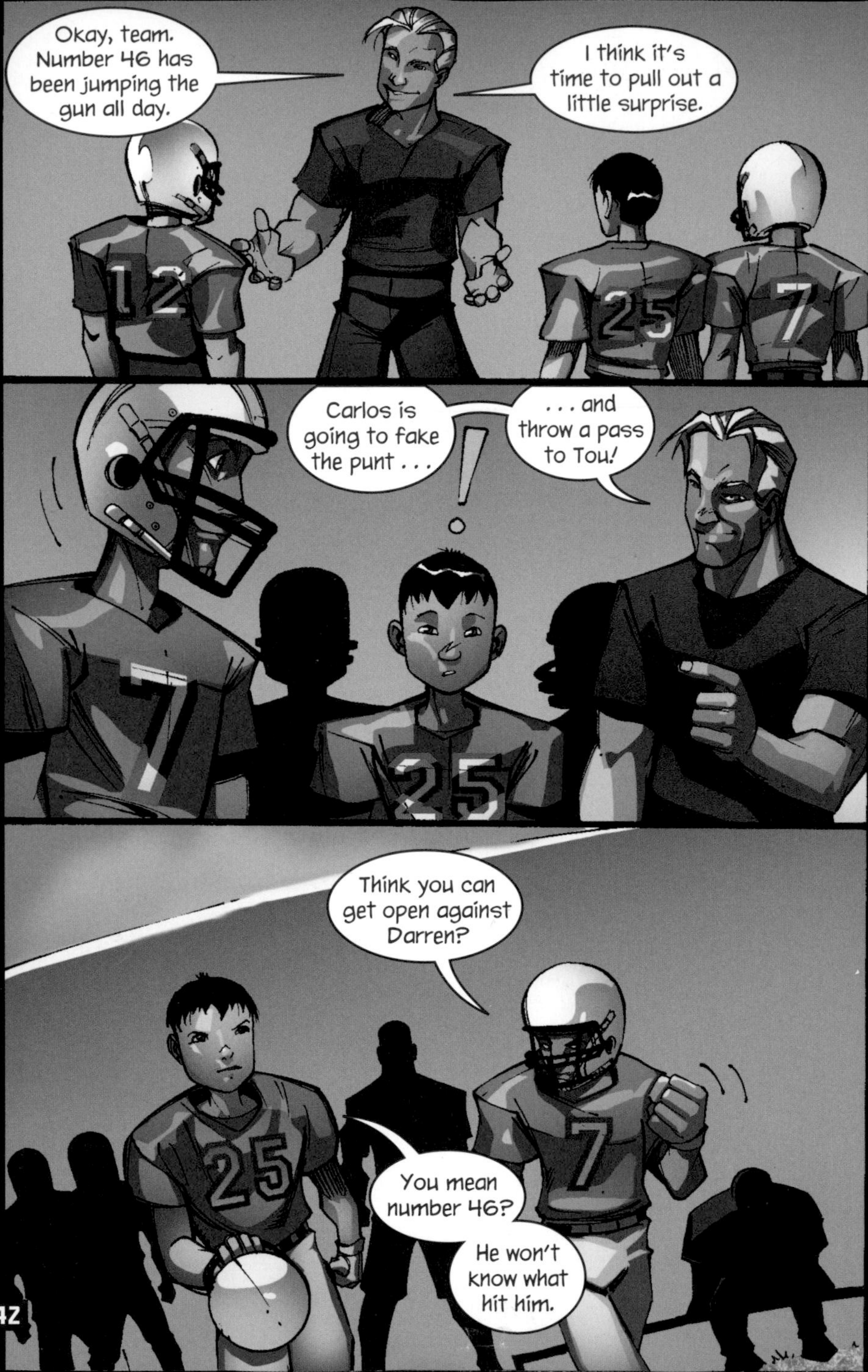
Okay, team. Number 46 has been jumping the gun all day.
I think it's time to pull out a little surprise.
Carlos is going to fake the punt . . .
. . . and throw a pass to Tou!
!
Think you can get open against Darren?
You mean number 46?
He won't know what hit him.

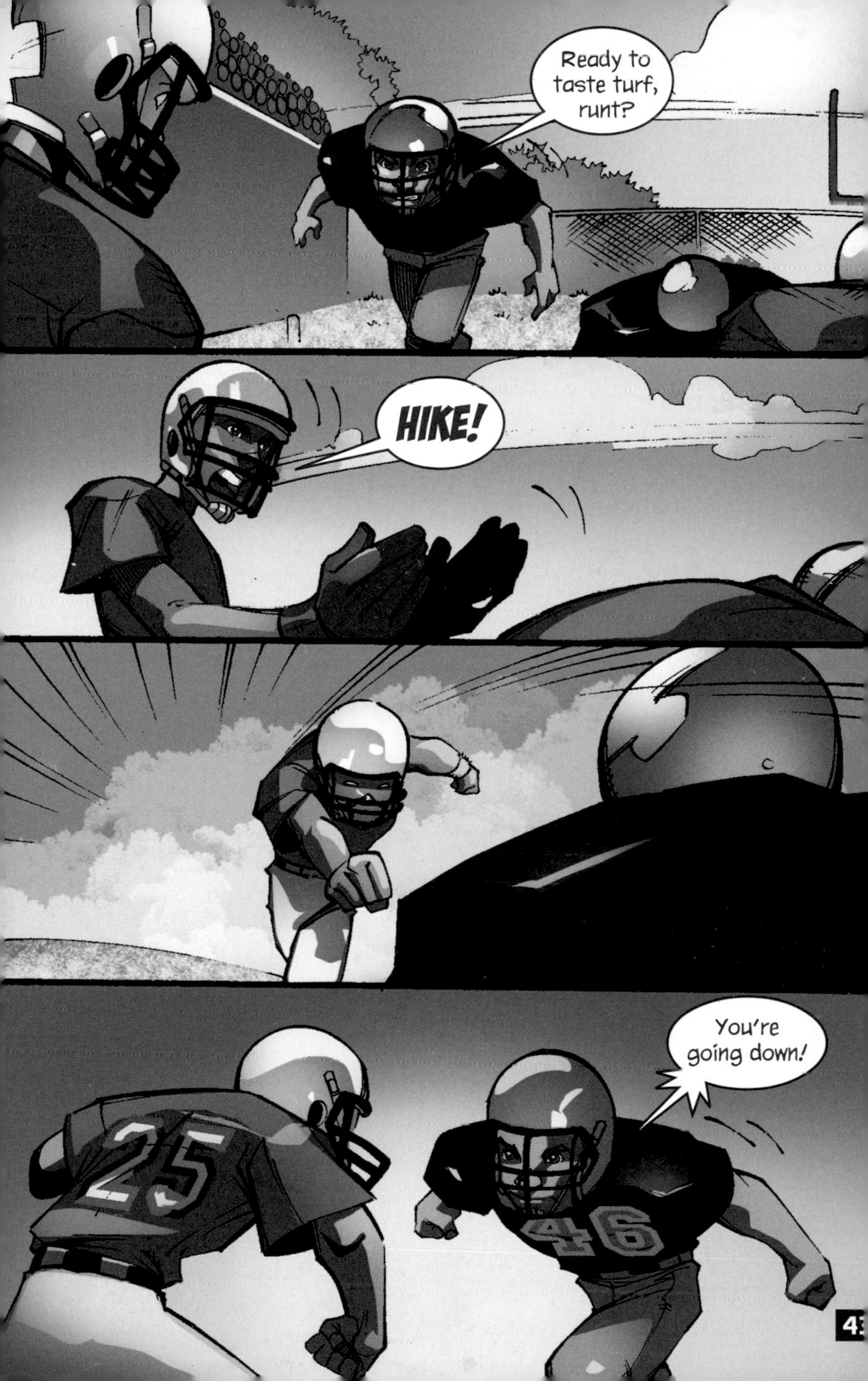
Ready to taste turf, runt?
HIKE!
You're going down!

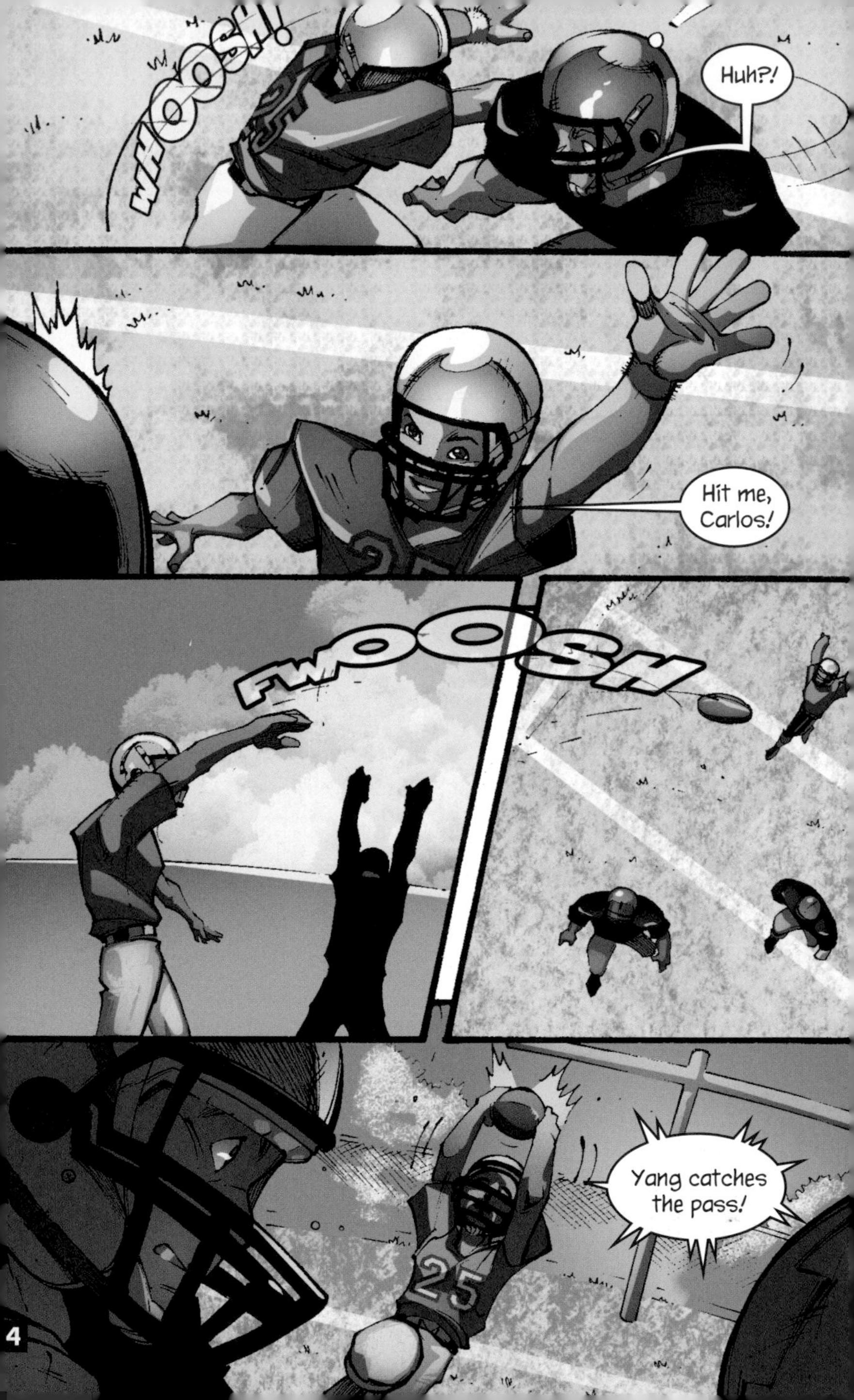
WHOOSH!
Huh?!
Hit me, Carlos!
FWOOSH
Yang catches the pass!

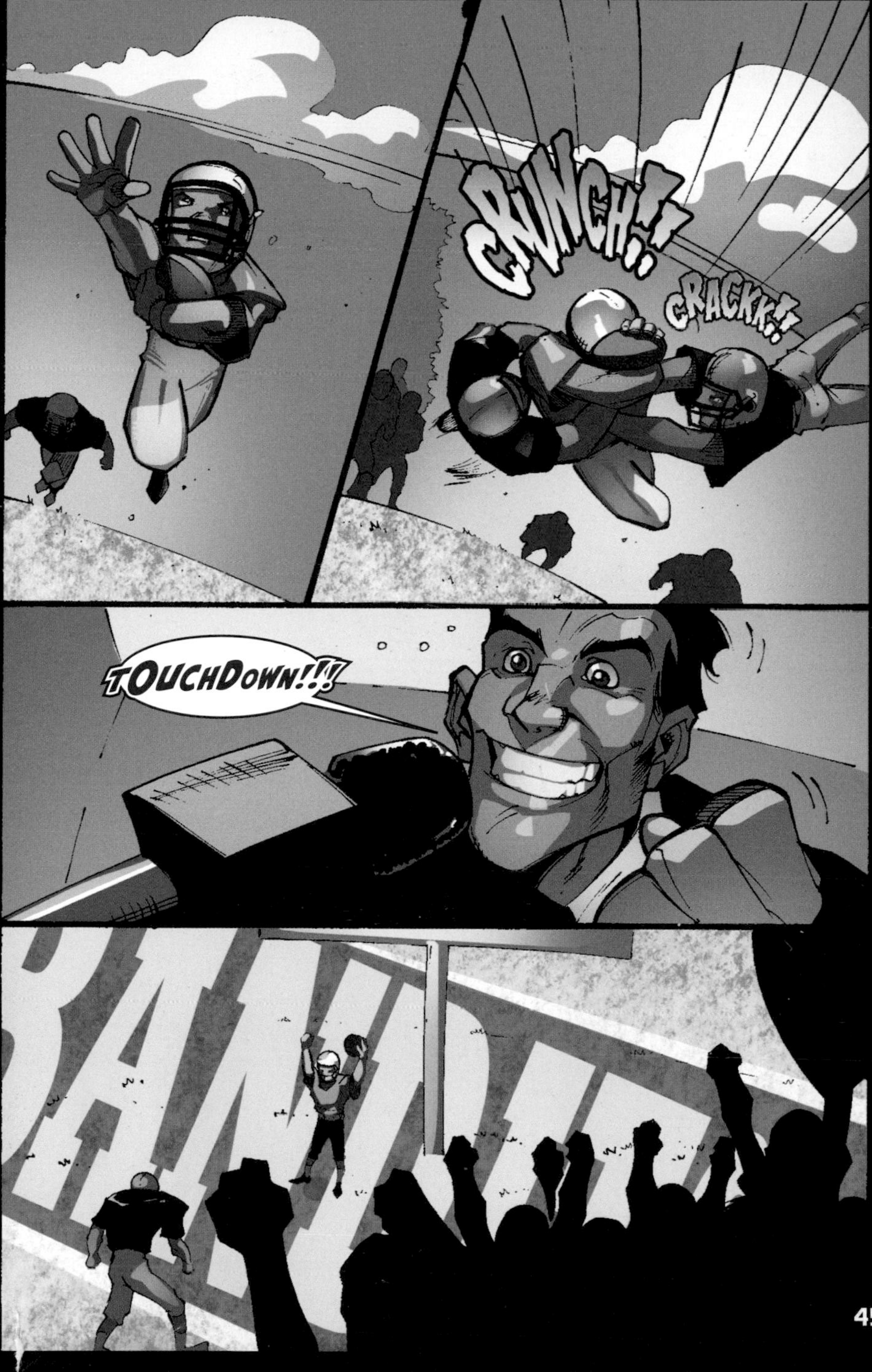
CRUNCH!!
CRACKK!!
TOUCHDOWN!!!

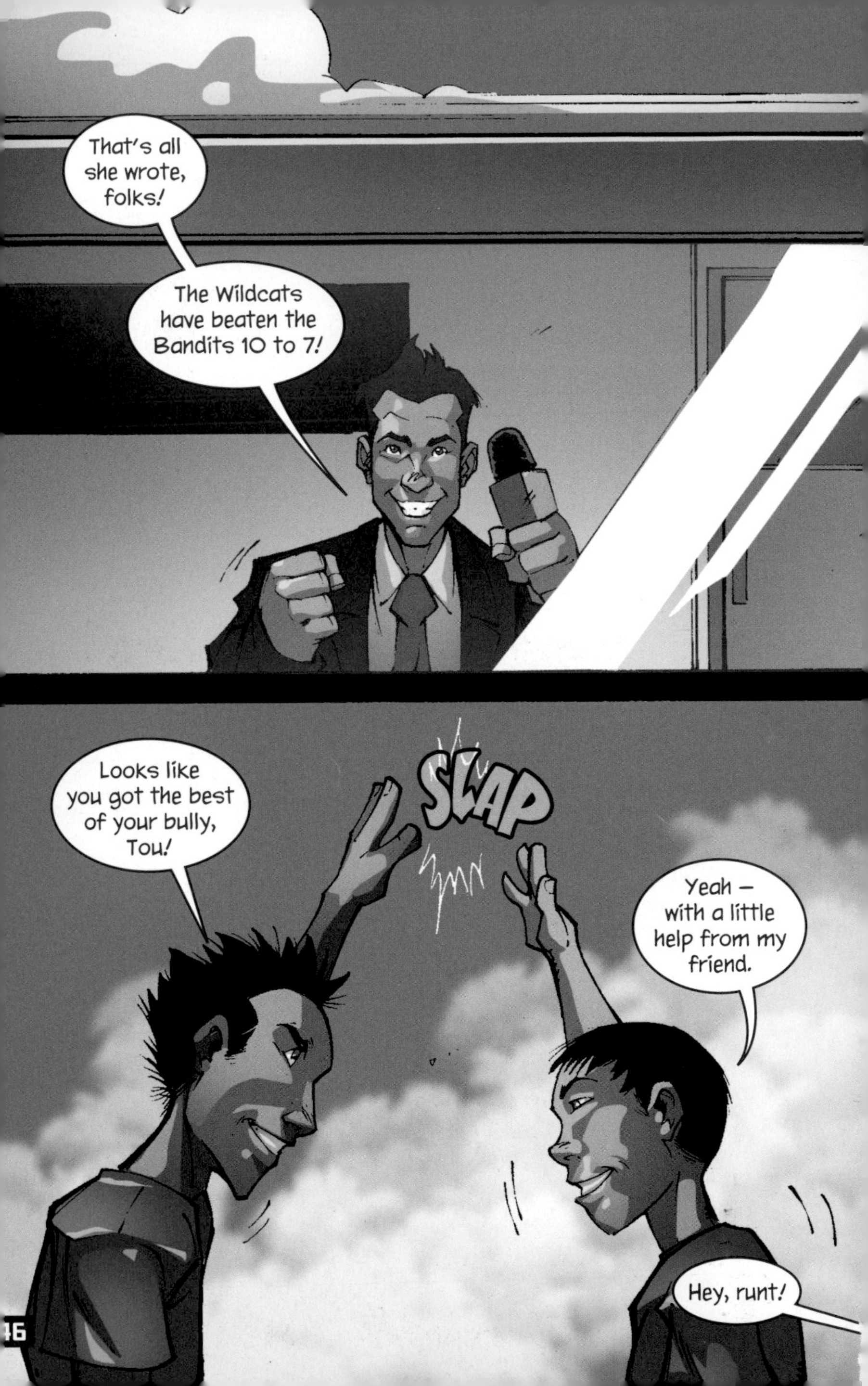
That's all she wrote, folks!
The Wildcats have beaten the Bandits 10 to 7!
Looks like you got the best of your bully, Tou!
SLAP
Yeah — with a little help from my friend.
Hey, runt!

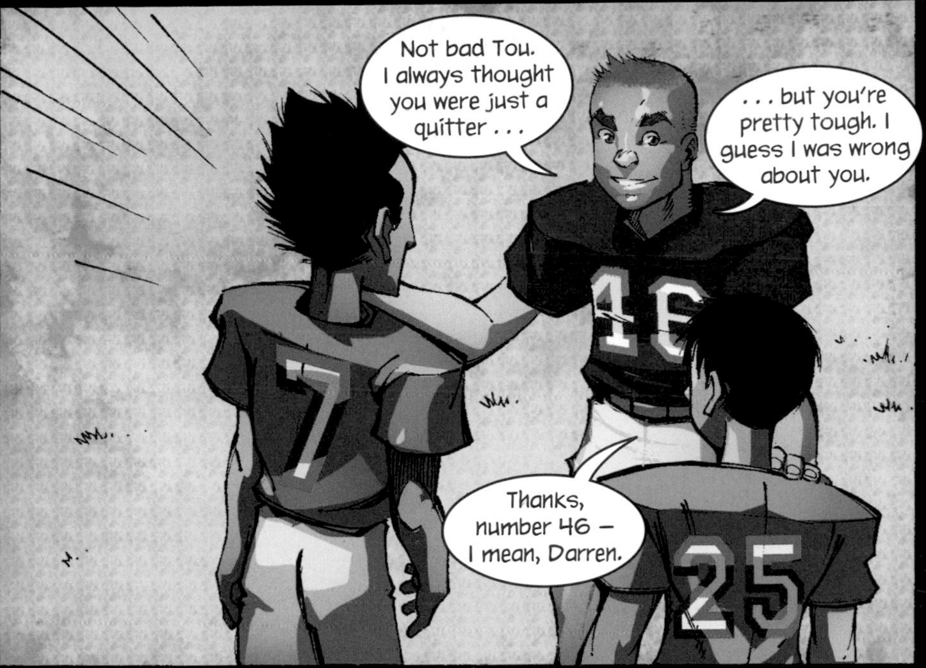
Not bad Tou. I always thought you were just a quitter . . .
. . . but you're pretty tough. I guess I was wrong about you.
Thanks, number 46 — I mean, Darren.

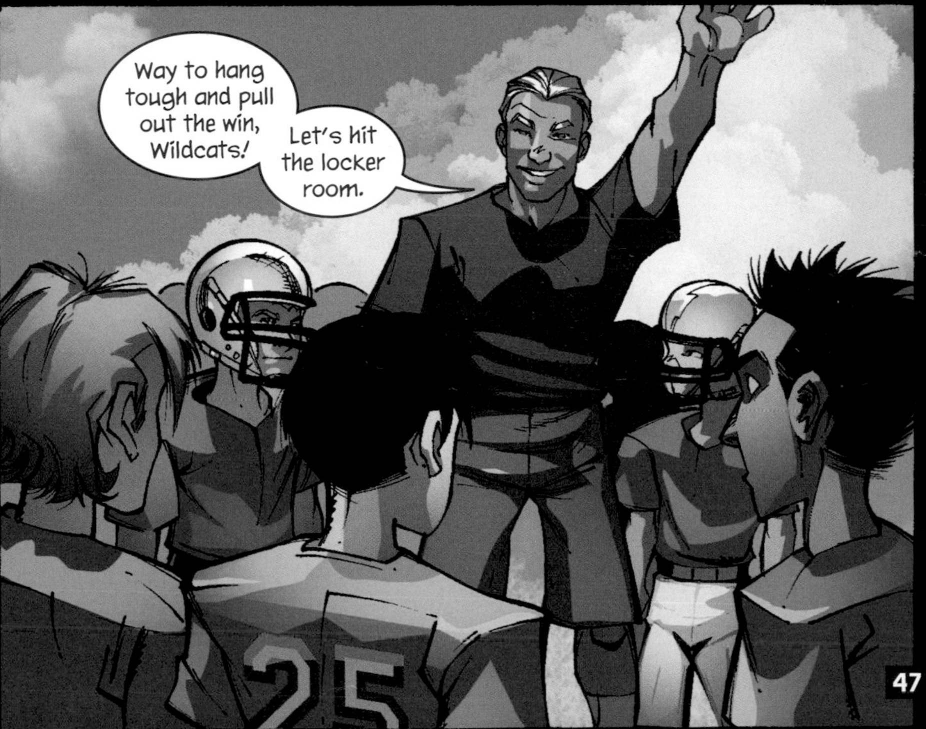
Way to hang tough and pull out the win, Wildcats!
Let's hit the locker room.

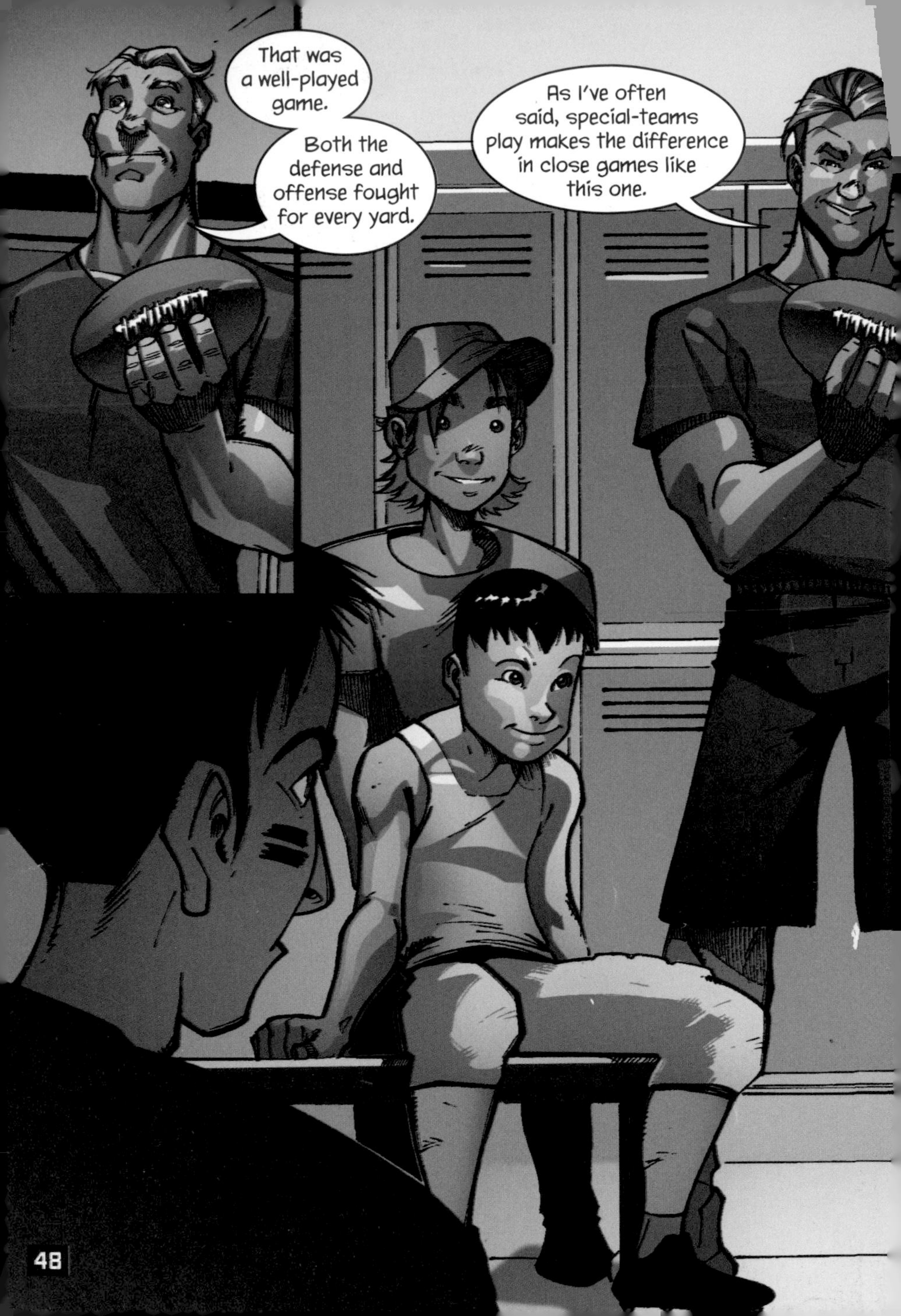
That was a well-played game.
Both the defense and offense fought for every yard.
As I've often said, special-teams play makes the difference in close games like this one.

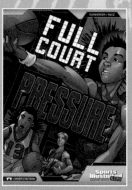

RICKY HOLDER IN:
REALITY CHECK

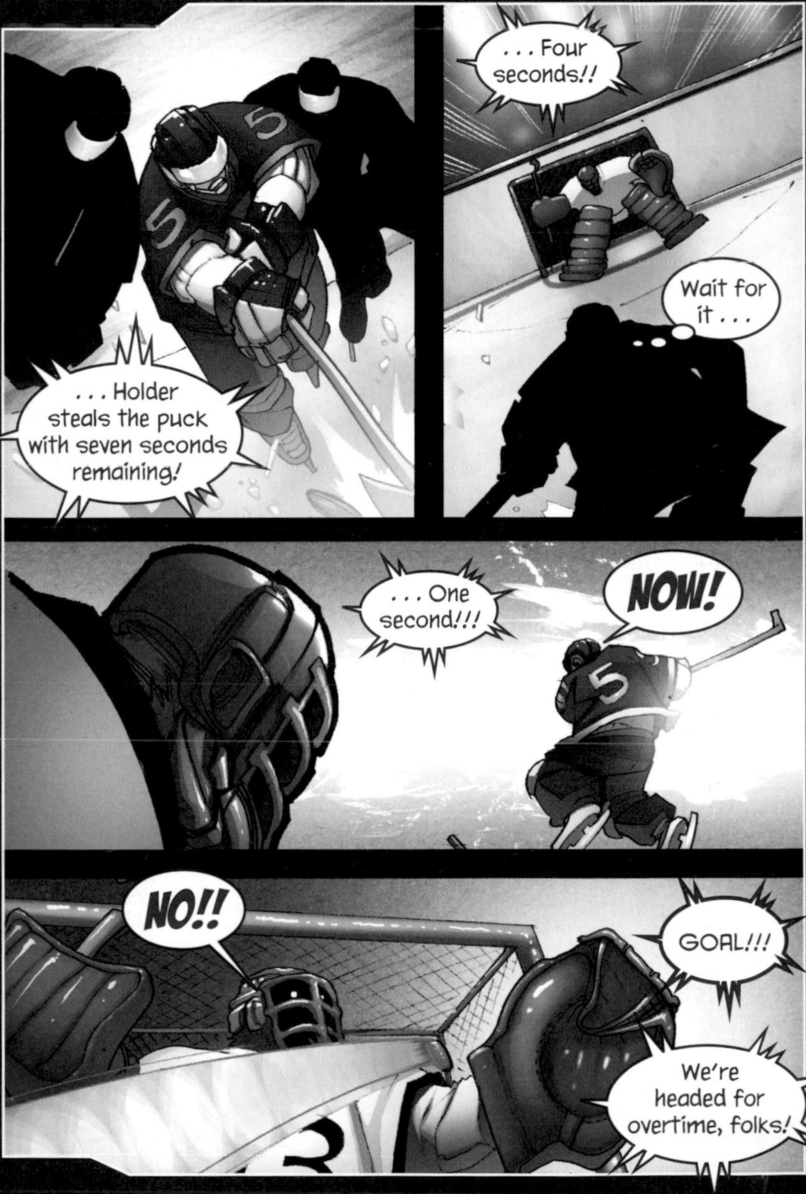
. . . Holder steals the puck with seven seconds remaining!
. . . Four seconds!!
Wait for it . . .
. . . One second!!!
NOW!
NO!!
GOAL!!!
We're headed for overtime, folks!

CREATORS

BLAKE A. HOENA › Author

Blake A. Hoena grew up in central Wisconsin. Later, he moved to Minnesota to pursue a Masters of Fine Arts degree in Creative Writing from Minnesota State University, Mankato. Since graduating, Blake has written more than thirty books and graphic novels for children. Blake currently lives in Minneapolis, Minnesota with his quirky dog, Zuki.

ALFONSO RUIZ › Illustrator

Alfonso Ruiz was born in 1975 in Macuspana, Tabasco in Mexico, where the temperature is just as hot as the sauce is. He became a comic book illustrator when he was 17 years old, and has worked on many Spanish graphic novels since then. Alfonso has also illustrated several English graphic novels, including retellings of *Dracula* and *Pinocchio*.

JORGE GONZALEZ › Colorist

Jorge Gonzalez was born in Monterrey, Mexico. Jorge began his career as a colorist for the graphic novel retellings of *The Time Machine* and *Journey to the Center of the Earth*. In 2006, Jorge helped establish Protobunker Studio, where he currently works as a colorist.

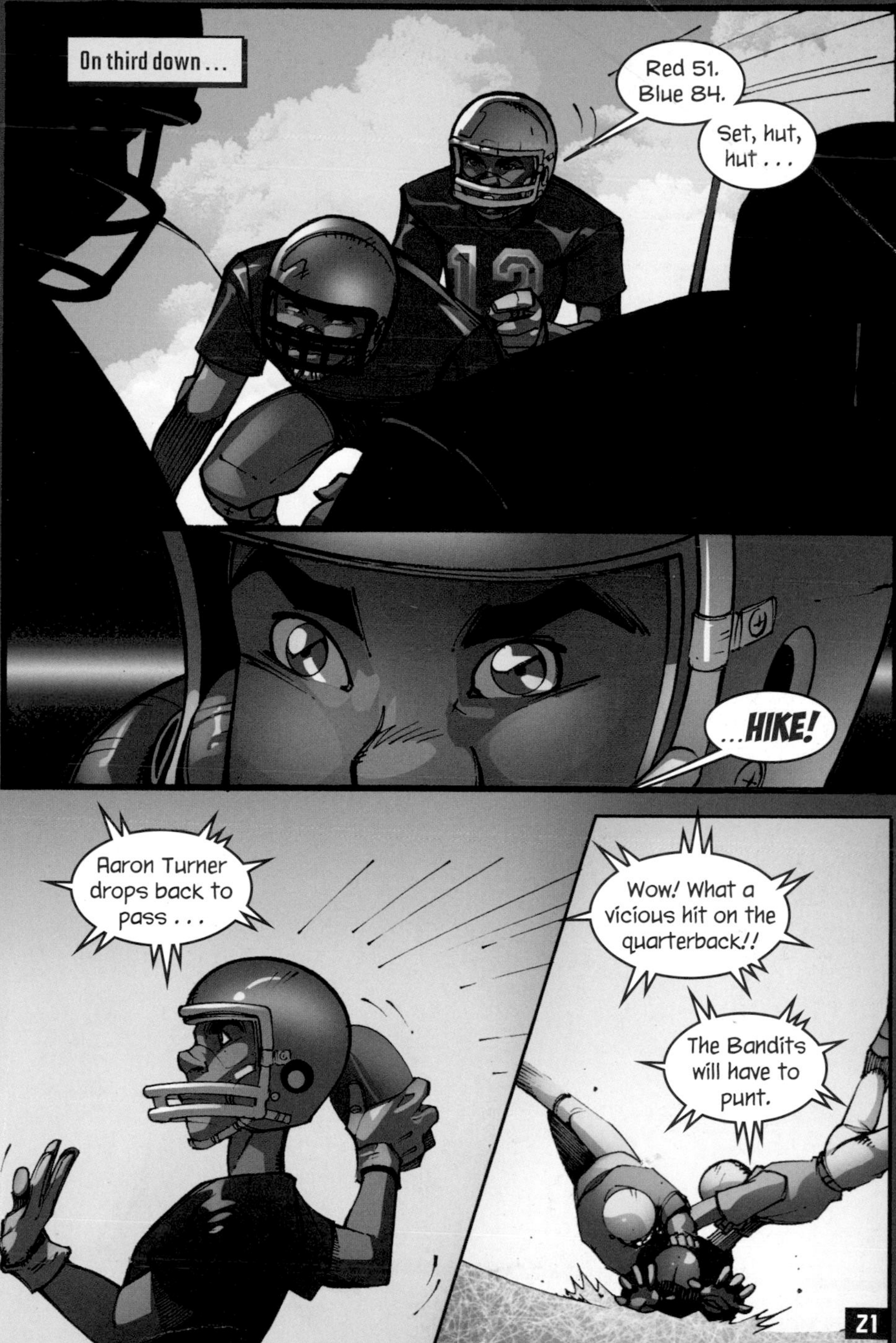

On third down . . .
Red 51. Blue 84.
Set, hut, hut . . .
. . . HIKE!
Aaron Turner drops back to pass . . .
Wow! What a vicious hit on the quarterback!!
The Bandits will have to punt.

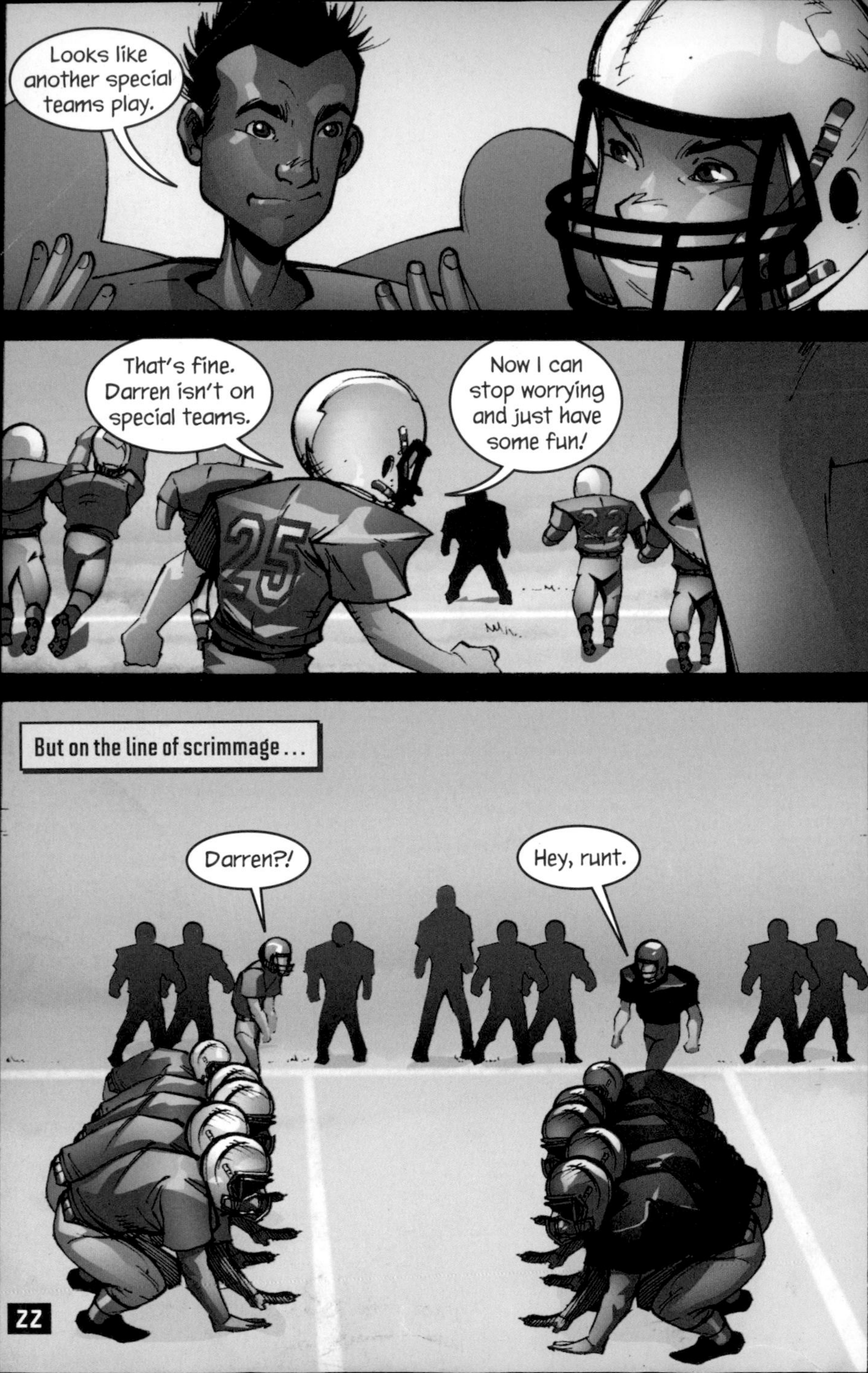
Looks like another special teams play.
That's fine. Darren isn't on special teams.
Now I can stop worrying and just have some fun!
But on the line of scrimmage . . .
Darren?!
Hey, runt.

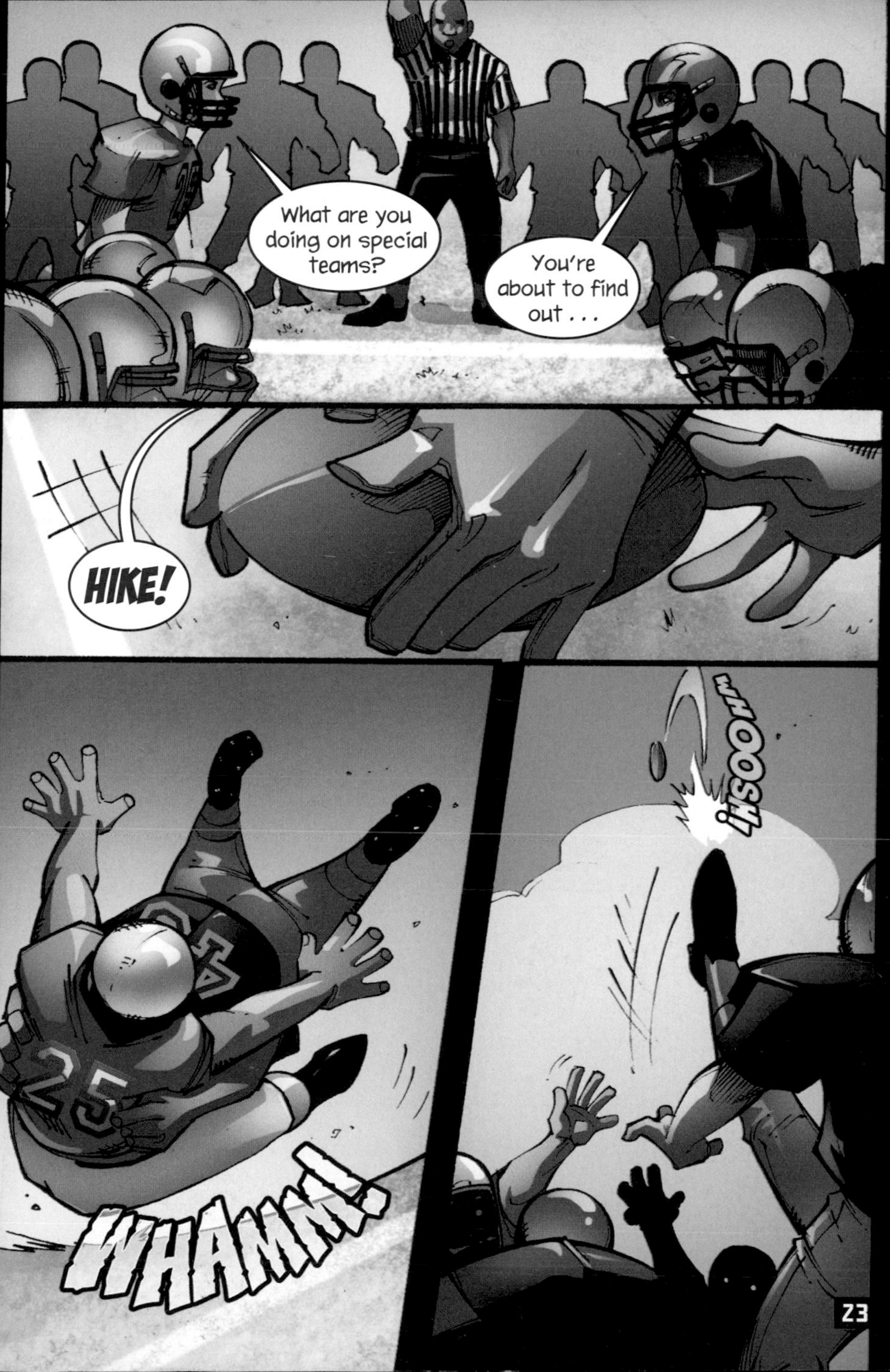

What are you doing on special teams?
You're about to find out . . .
HIKE!
WHAMM!
WHOOSH!

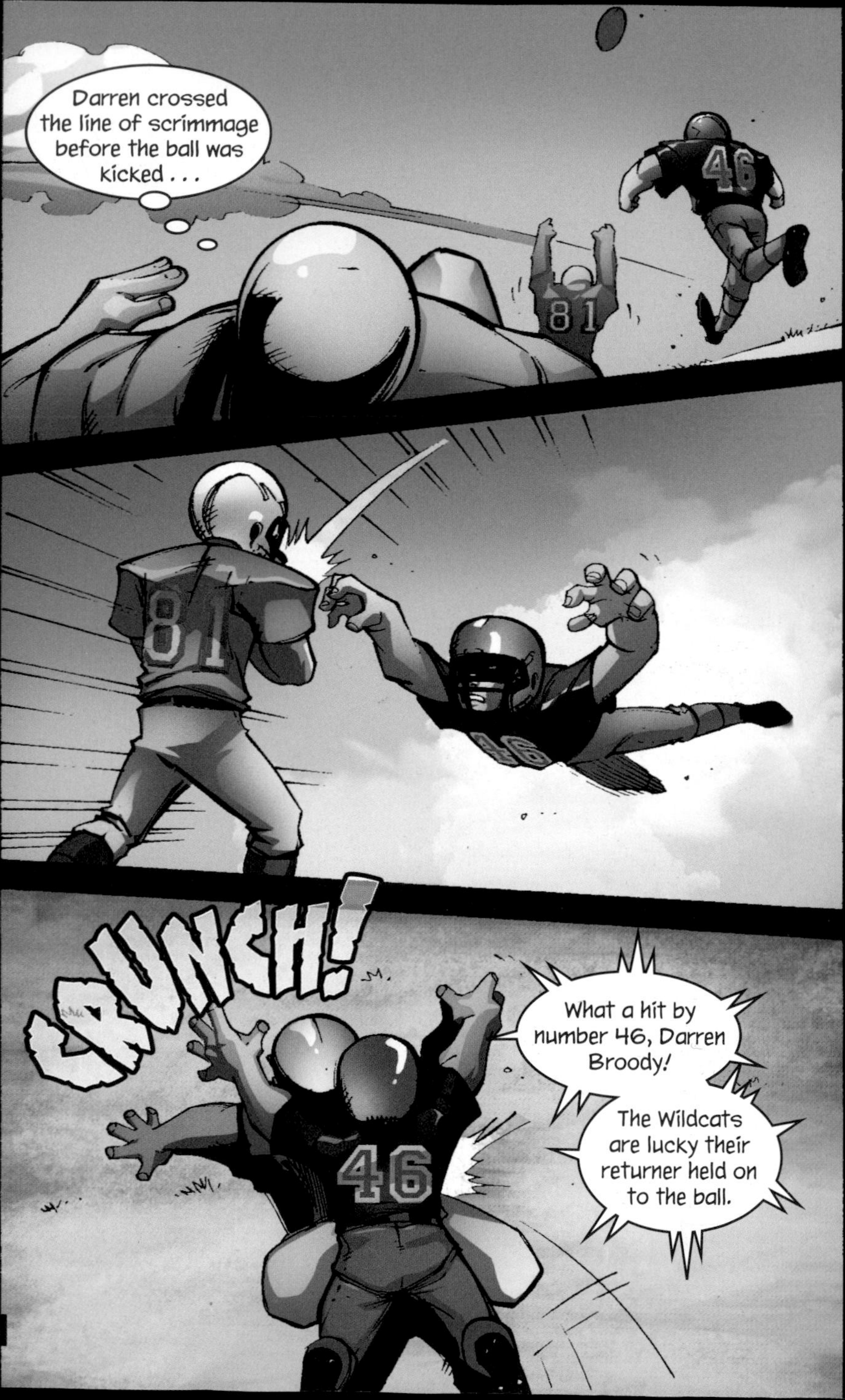
Darren crossed the line of scrimmage before the ball was kicked . . .
CRUNCH!
What a hit by number 46, Darren Broody!
The Wildcats are lucky their returner held on to the ball.

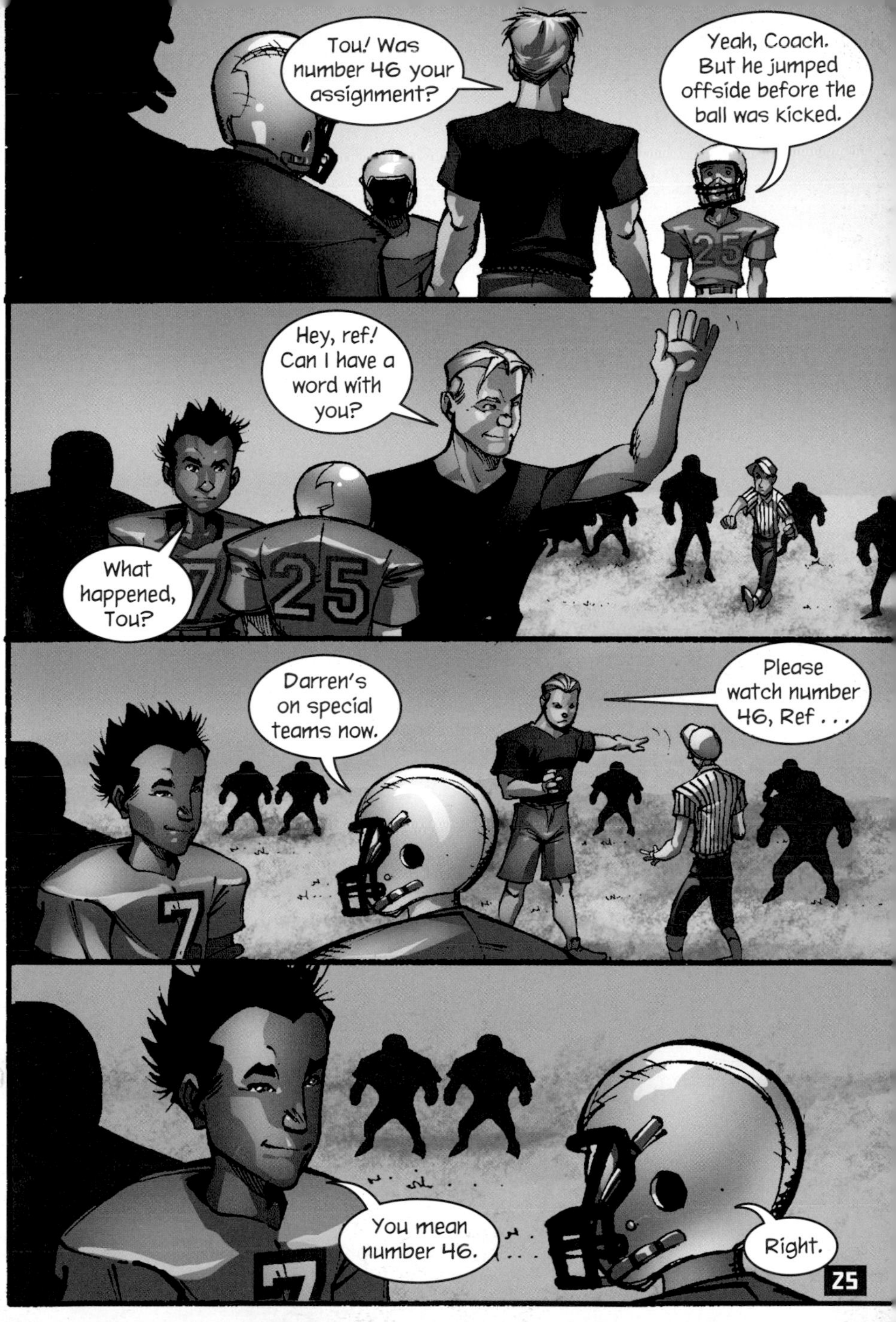
Tou! Was number 46 your assignment?
Yeah, Coach. But he jumped offside before the ball was kicked.
Hey, ref! Can I have a word with you?
What happened, Tou?
Darren's on special teams now.
Please watch number 46, Ref . . .
You mean number 46.
Right.

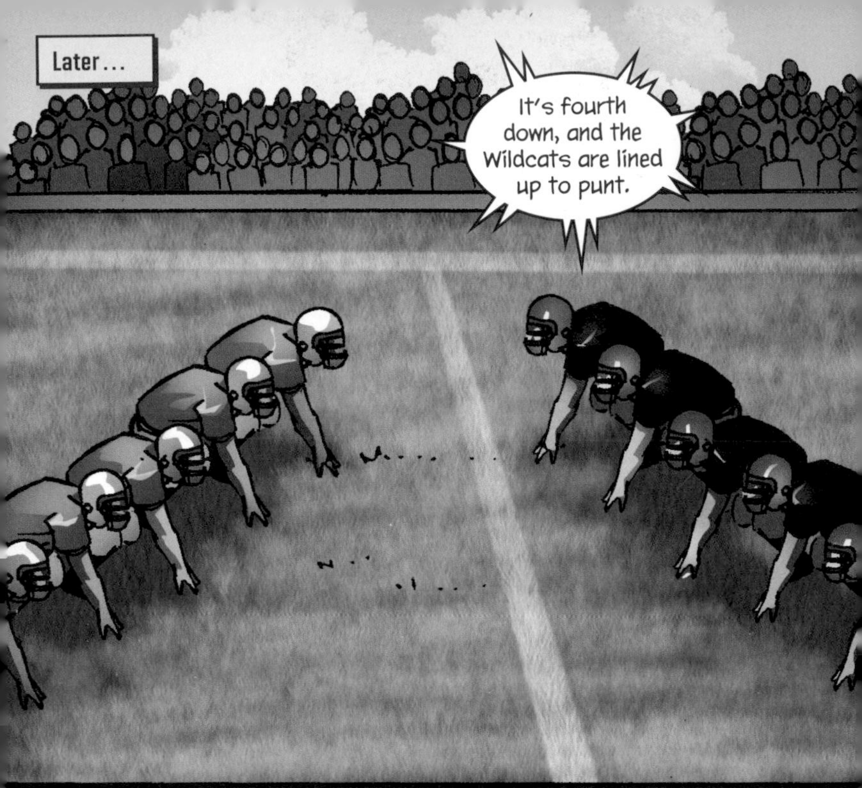
Later...
It's fourth down, and the Wildcats are lined up to punt.

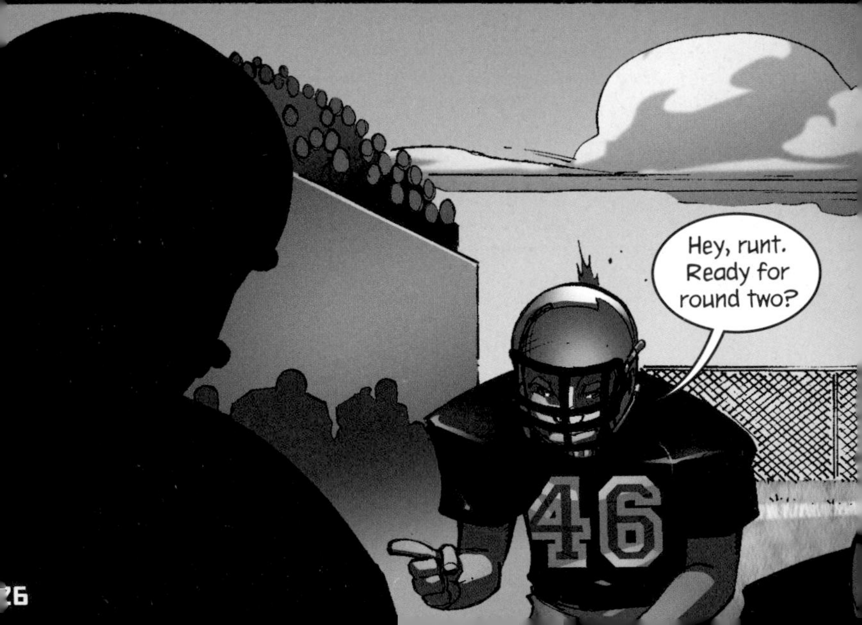
Hey, runt. Ready for round two?

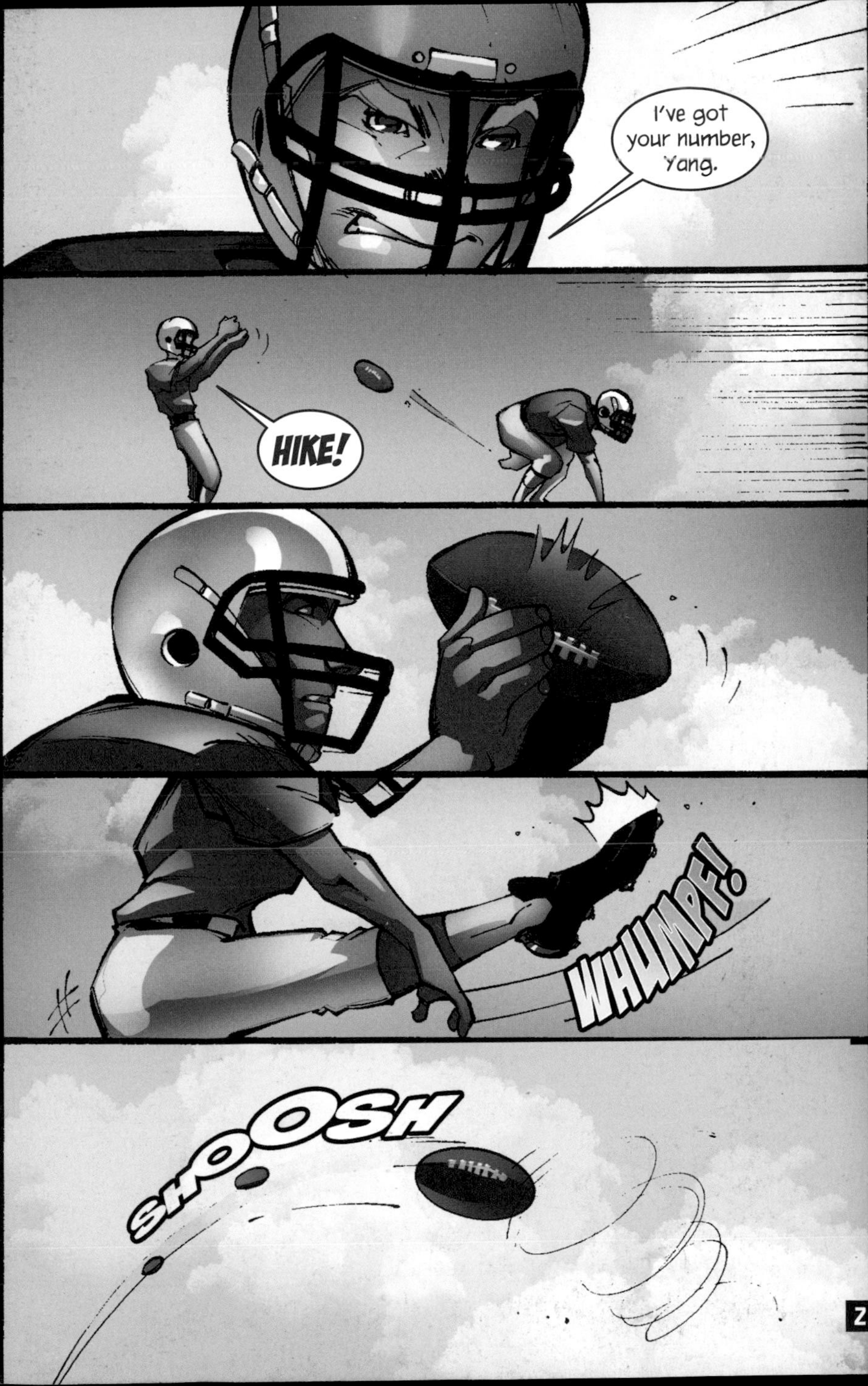
I've got your number, Yang.
HIKE!
WHUMPF!
SHOOOSH

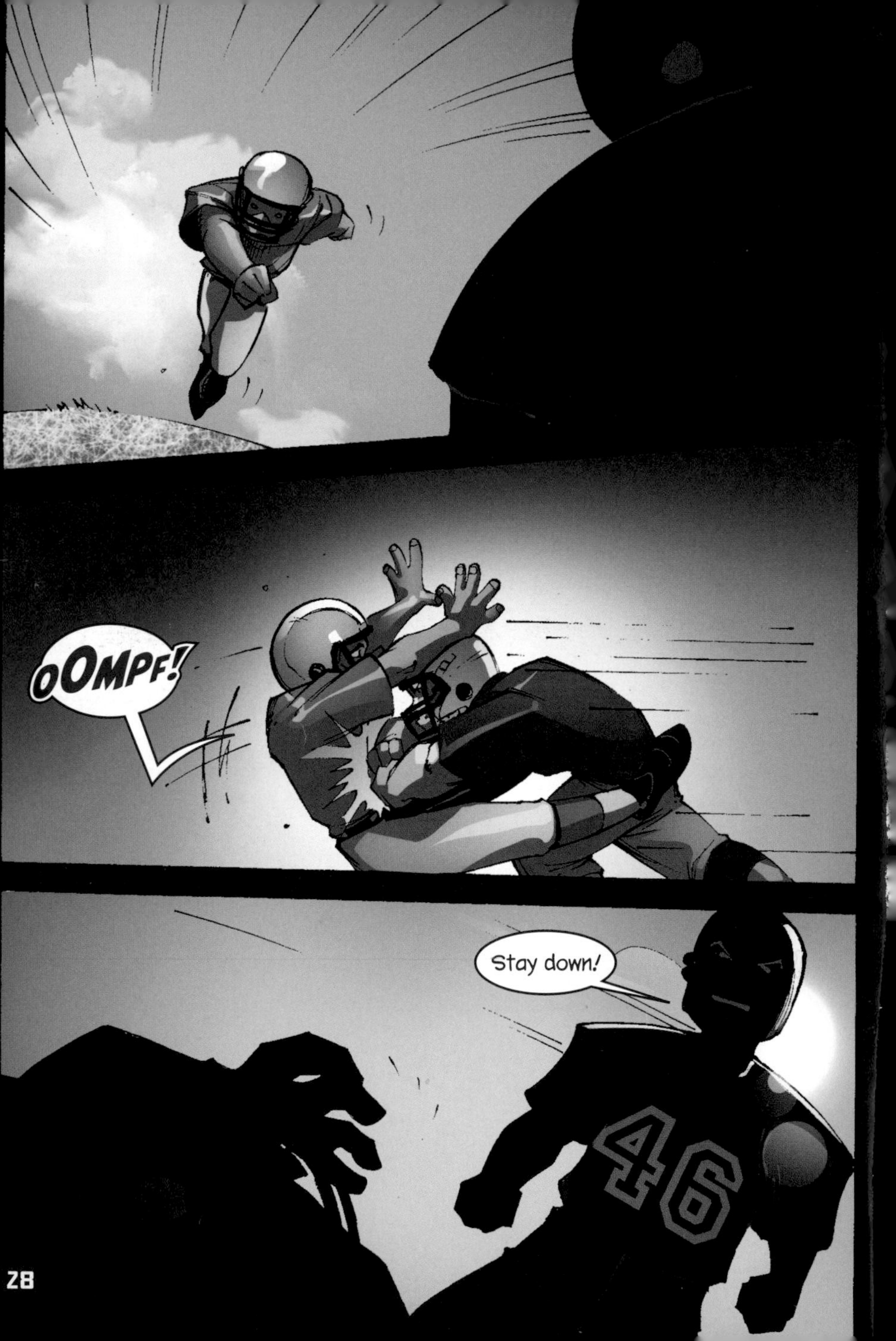
OOMPF!
Stay down!
46

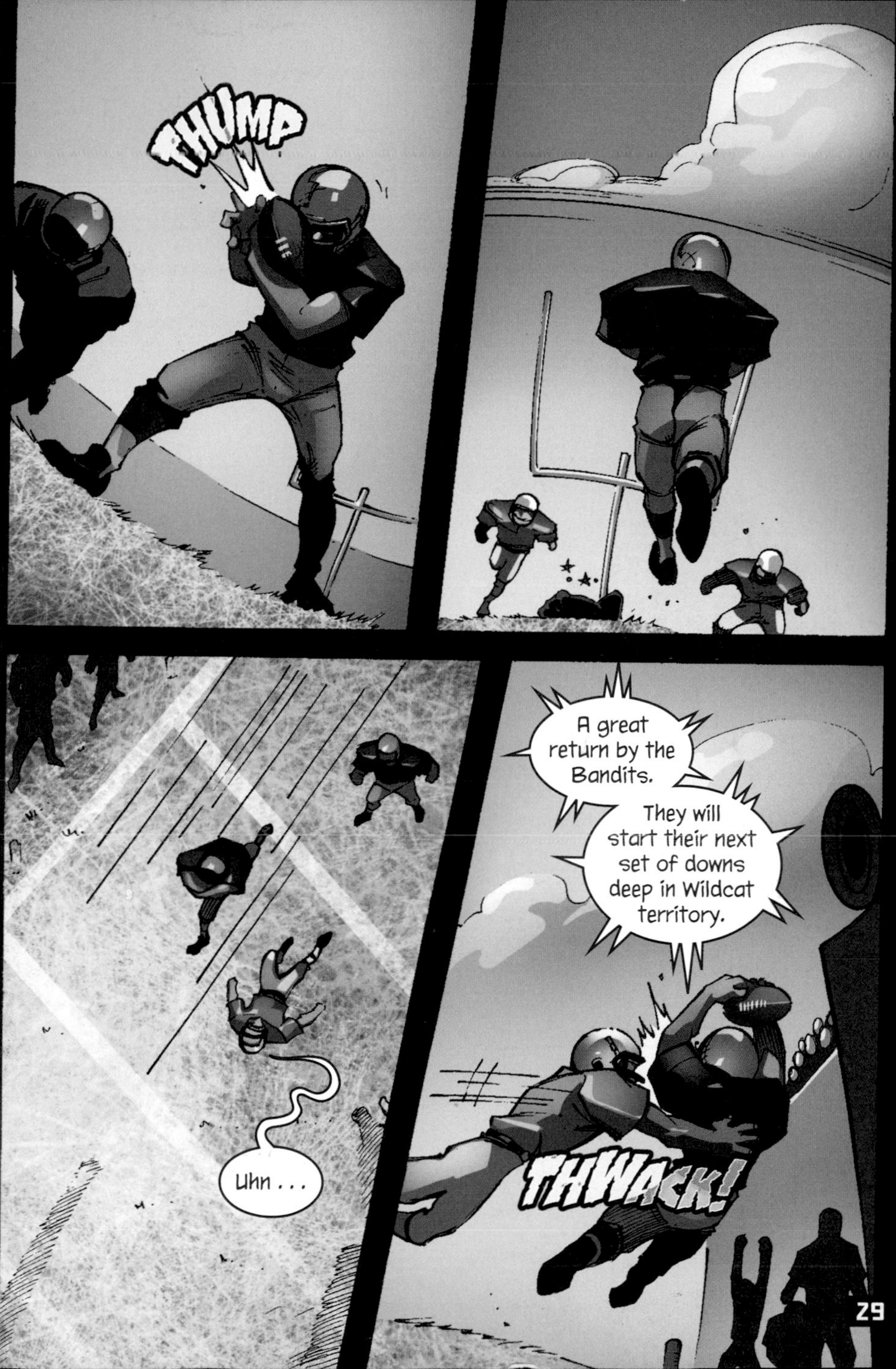
THUMP
Uhn . . .
A great return by the Bandits.
They will start their next set of downs deep in Wildcat territory.
THWACK!

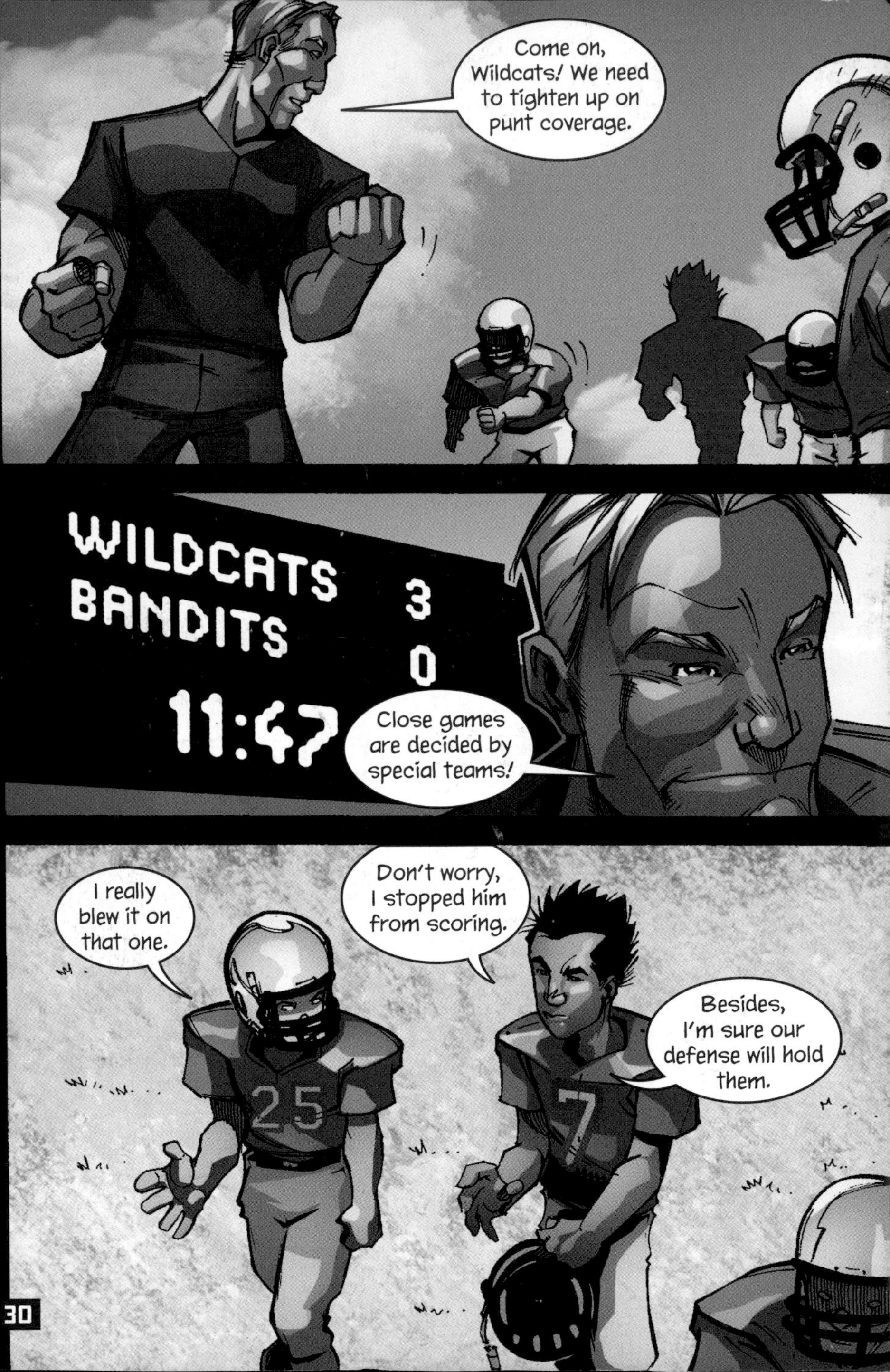
Come on, Wildcats! We need to tighten up on punt coverage.
WILDCATS 3
BANDITS 0
11:47
Close games are decided by special teams!
I really blew it on that one.
Don't worry, I stopped him from scoring.
Besides, I'm sure our defense will hold them.
25
7

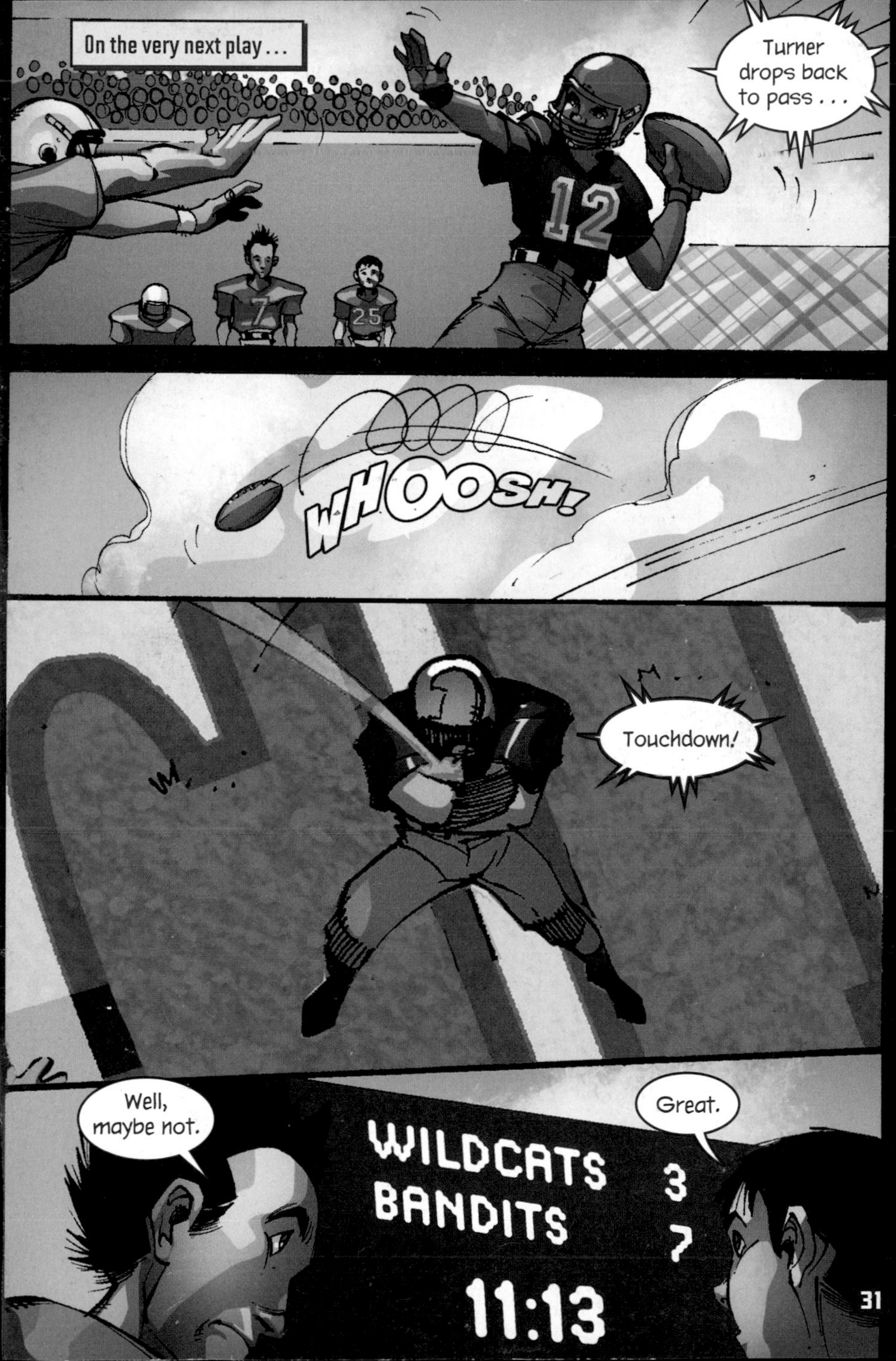
On the very next play . . .
Turner drops back to pass . . .
WHOOSH!
Touchdown!
Well, maybe not.
WILDCATS 3
BANDITS 7
11:13
Great.

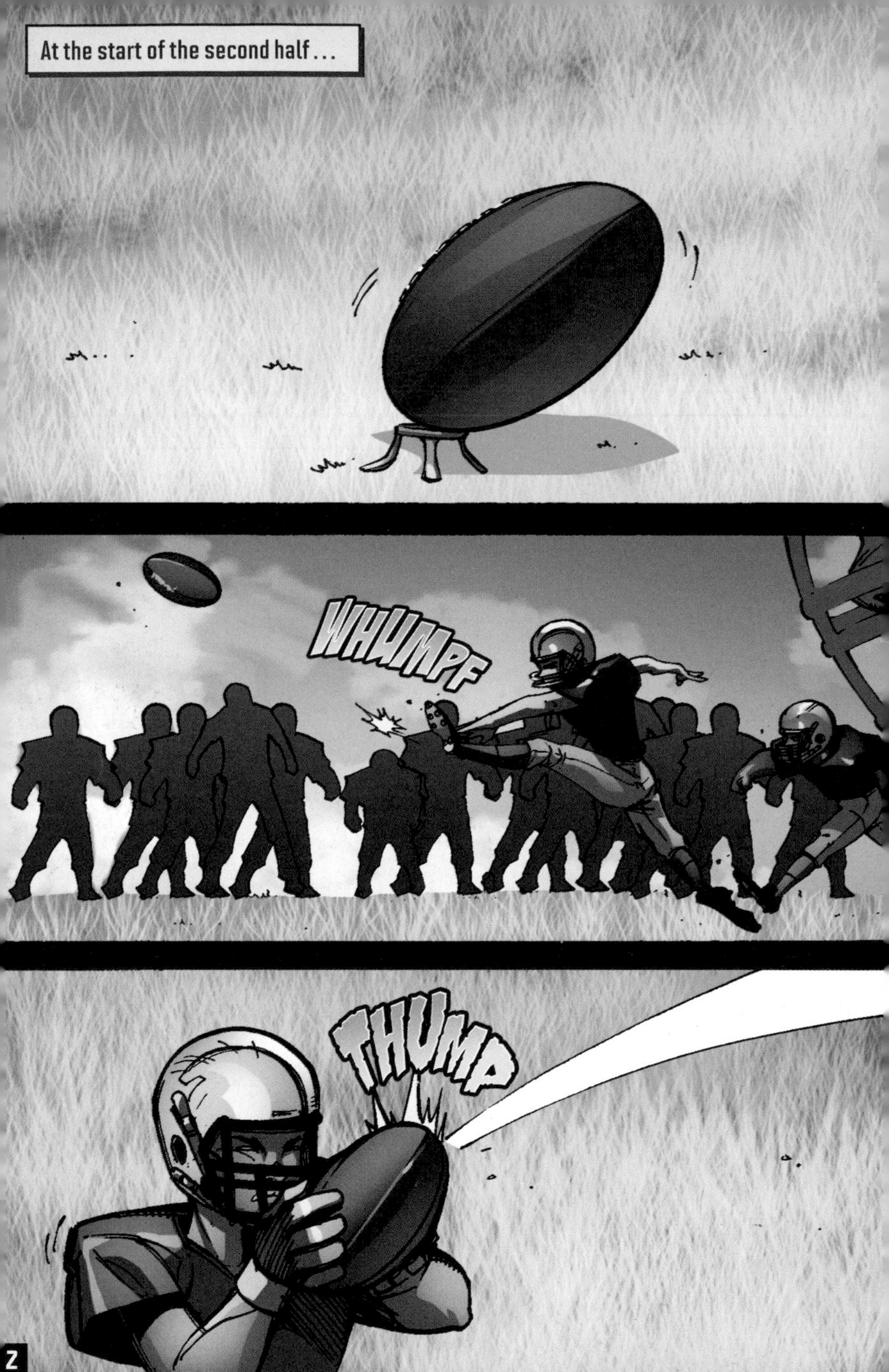
At the start of the second half . . .
WHUMPF
THUMP

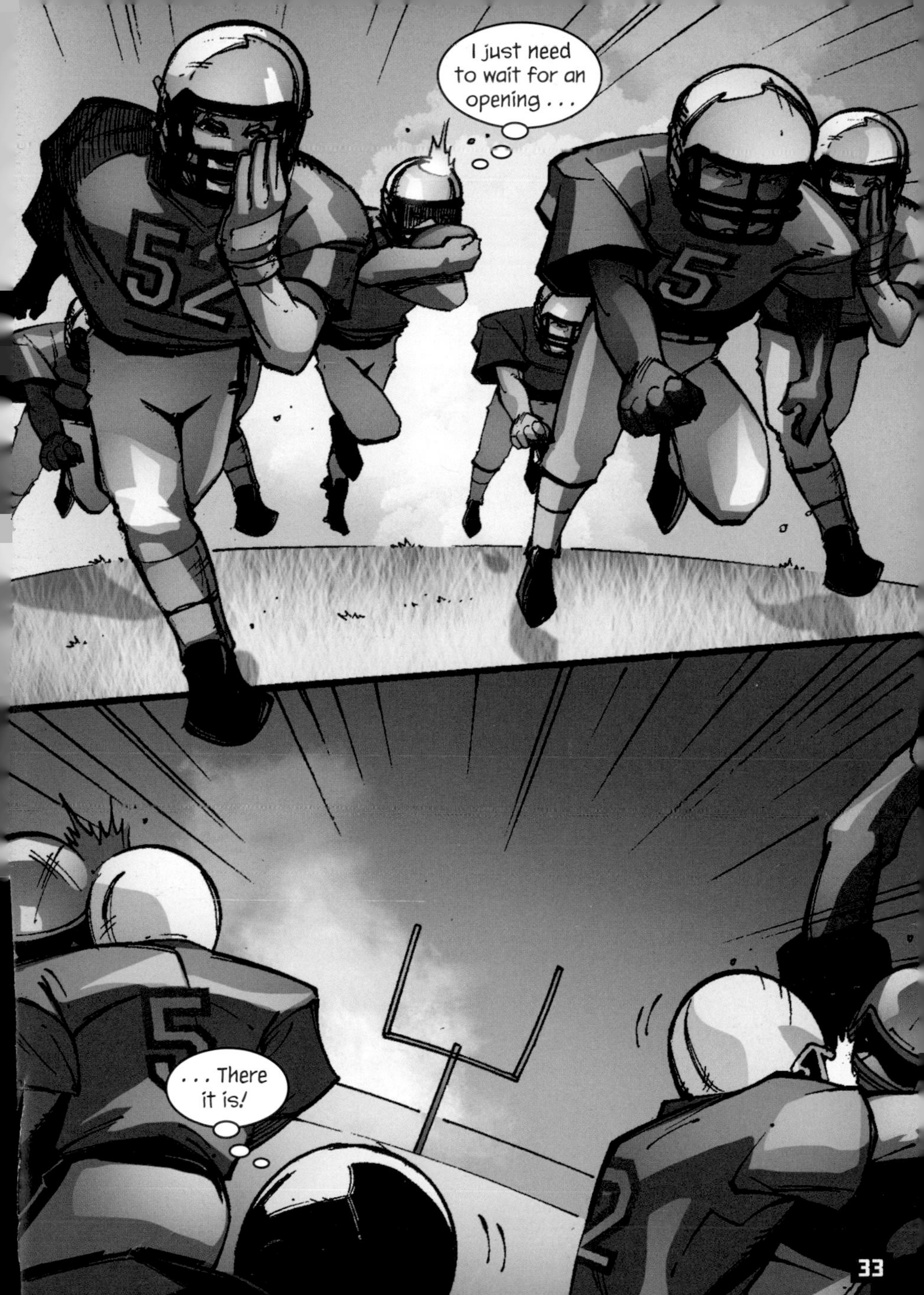
I just need to wait for an opening . . .
. . . There it is!

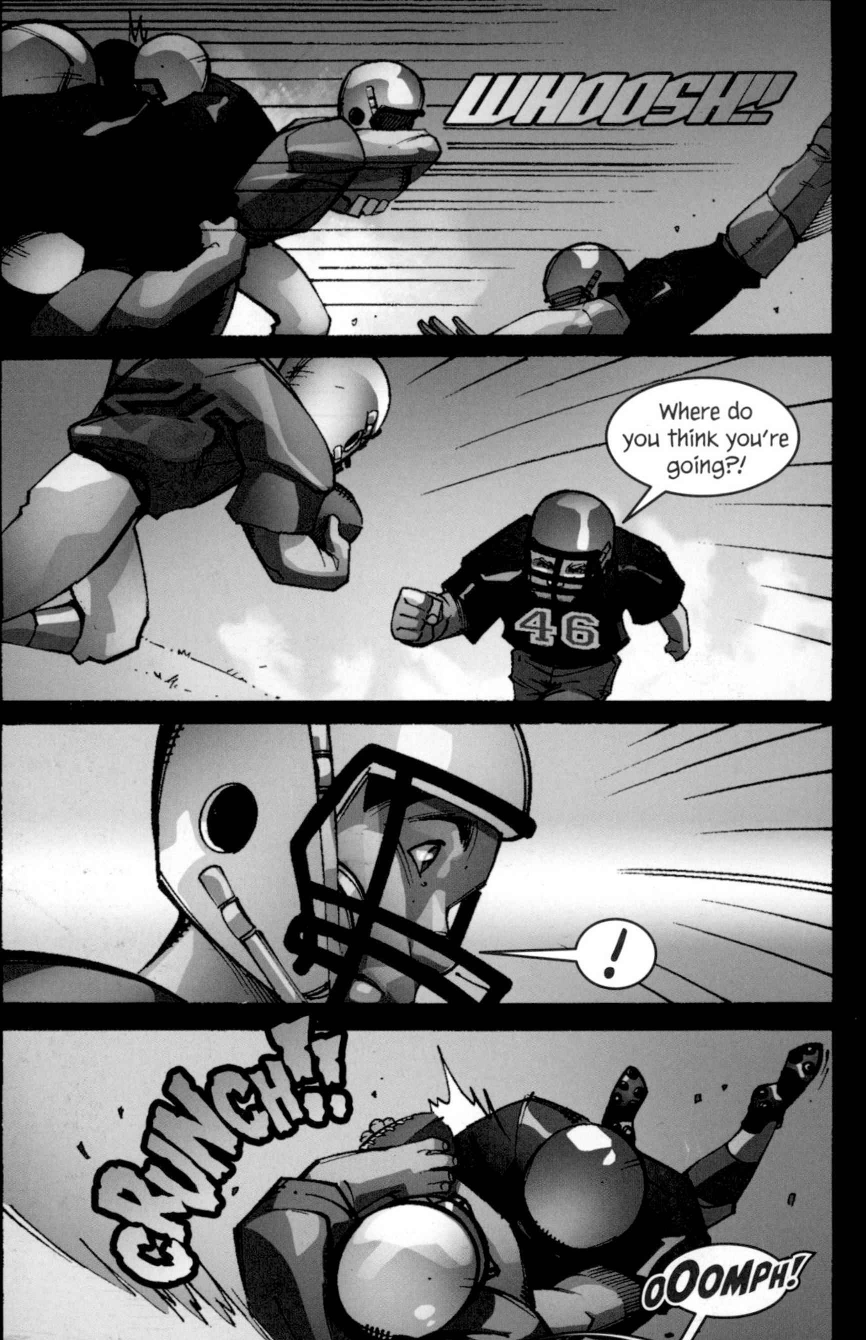
WHOOSH!!
Where do you think you're going?!
!
CRUNCH!!
OOOMPH!

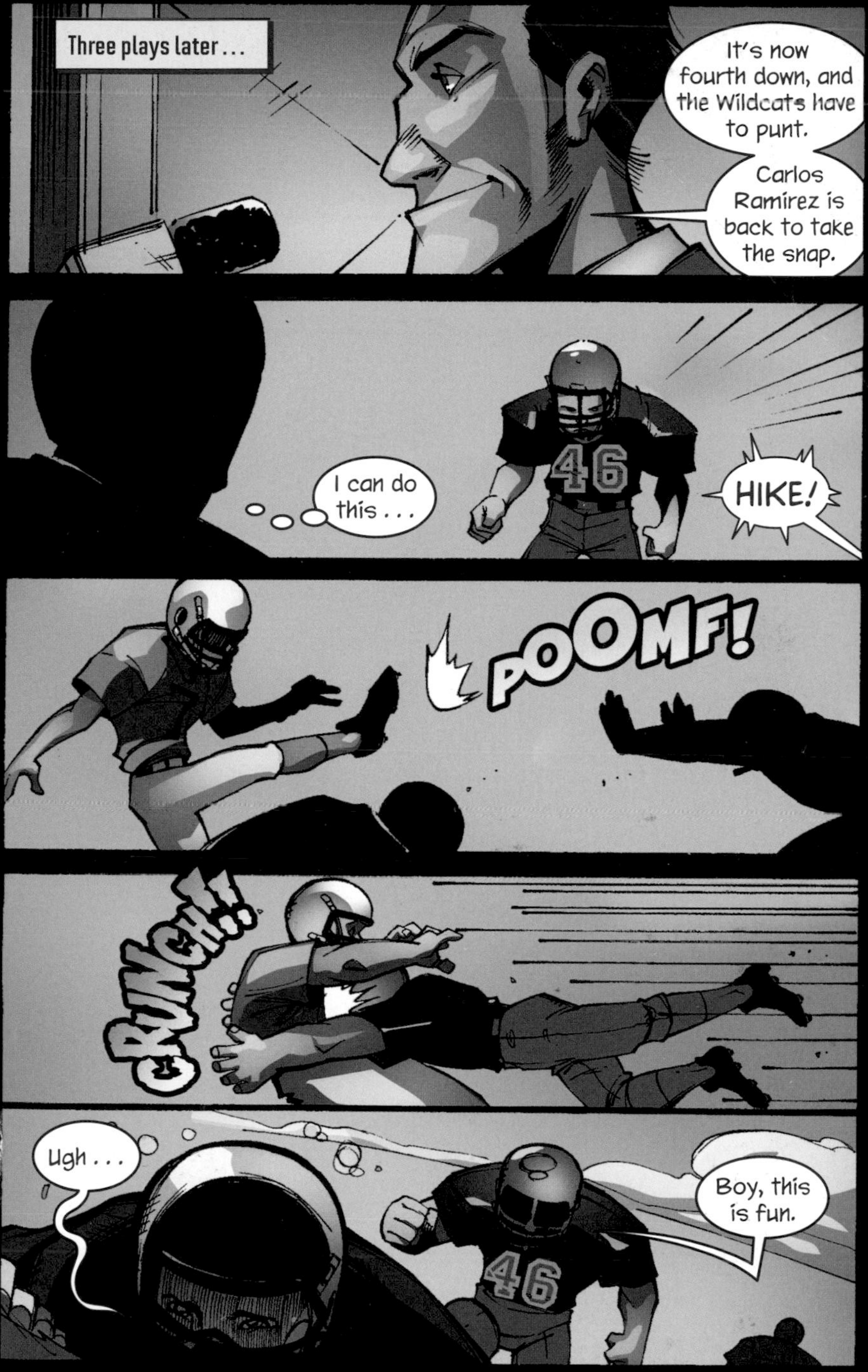
Three plays later . . .
It's now fourth down, and the Wildcats have to punt.
Carlos Ramirez is back to take the snap.
I can do this . . .
HIKE!
POOMF!
CRUNCH!!
Ugh . . .
Boy, this is fun.

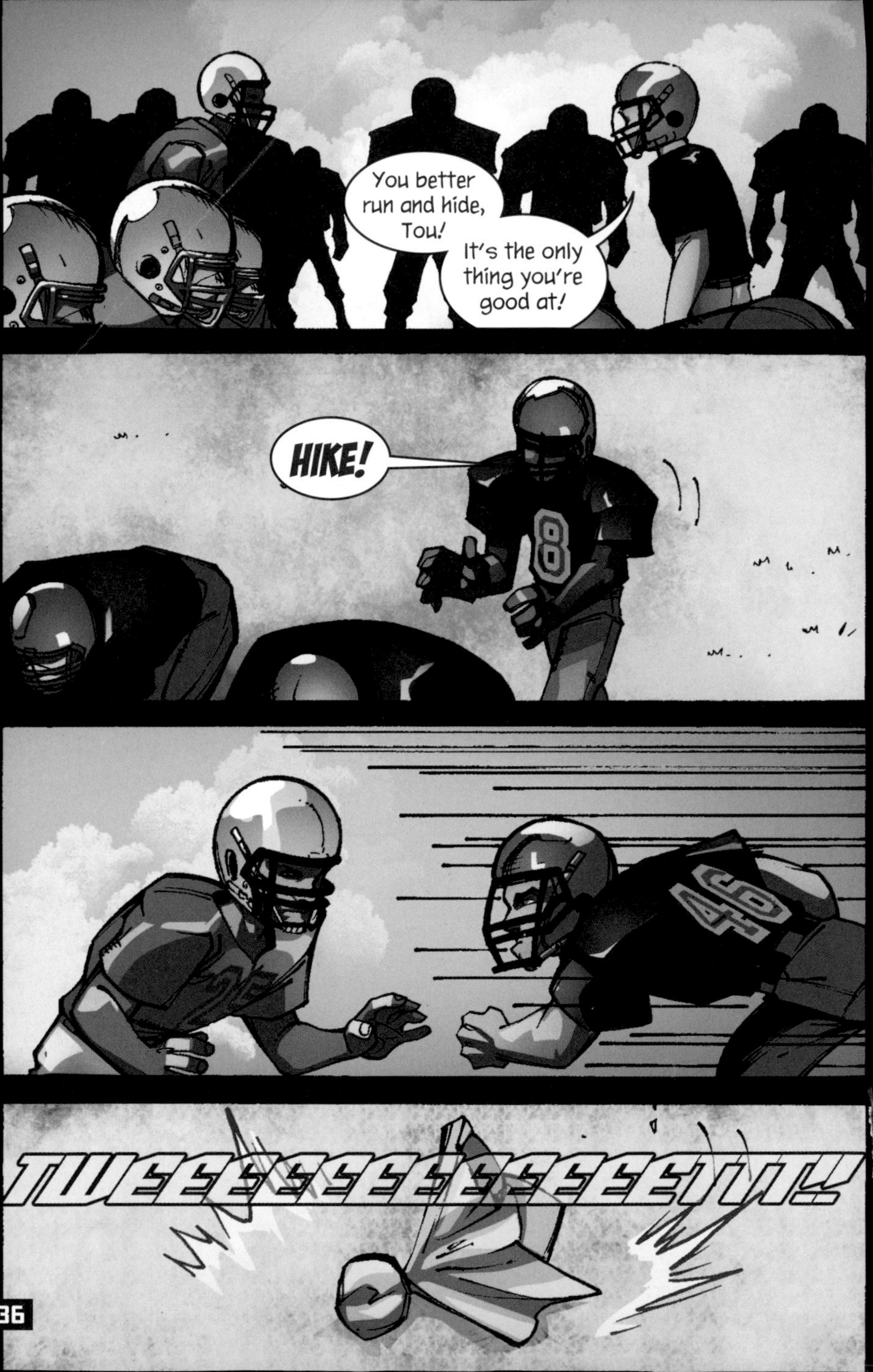
You better run and hide, Tou!
It's the only thing you're good at!
HIKE!
TWEEEEEEEEEEEEEEEET!!